TALKING TOAD
THE COMPLETE ADVENTURES
OF THE GADGET MAN, VOLUME 1

TALKING TOAD

THE COMPLETE ADVENTURES OF THE GADGET MAN, VOLUME 1

LESTER DENT

PRIMARY ILLUSTRATORS:
ALBERT MICALE
WILSON SCRUGGS

ALTUS PRESS
2023

PUBLISHING HISTORY

"Introduction" appears here for the first time. Copyright © 2023 Will Murray. All Rights Reserved.

© Condé Nast. ™ Condé Nast. Used with permission. "Talking Toad" originally published in *Crime Busters* magazine (November 1937).

© Condé Nast. ™ Condé Nast. Used with permission. "Death in Boxes" originally published in *Crime Busters* magazine (December 1937).

© Condé Nast. ™ Condé Nast. Used with permission. "Funny Faces" originally published in *Crime Busters* magazine (January 1938).

© Condé Nast. ™ Condé Nast. Used with permission. "The Scared Swamp" originally published in *Crime Busters* magazine (February 1938).

© Condé Nast. ™ Condé Nast. Used with permission. "Windjam" originally published in *Crime Busters* magazine (March 1938).

© Condé Nast. ™ Condé Nast. Used with permission. "The Little Mud Men" originally published in *Crime Busters* magazine (April 1938).

Restored texts copyright Condé Nast 2023.

THANKS TO

Christopher Wood, Elizabeth E. Engel, and the Lester Dent Collection at the State Historical Society of Missouri

TALKING TOAD

THE COMPLETE ADVENTURES OF THE GADGET MAN, VOLUME 1

LESTER DENT

PRIMARY ILLUSTRATORS:
ALBERT MICALE
WILSON SCRUGGS

ALTUS

ALTUS PRESS
2023

TABLE OF CONTENTS

INTRODUCTION

B OTH THE SHADOW'S creator Walter B. Gibson and his editor, John L. Nanovic, claimed to have conceived the idea that ultimately led to the creation of *Crime Busters*, and indirectly Lester Dent's Gadget Man series.

Street and Smith was searching for a new type of magazine, one that would showcase a strong hero, like *The Shadow* or *Doc Savage*. But in the Roosevelt Recession of 1937-38, new titles were a risky venture.

Gibson's idea was a "seed" magazine featuring three new heroes by top S&S writers. If any one grew popular, his thinking went, that character could be spun off into his own title and replaced by a new candidate.

> "I was talking to [S&S Business Manager Henry] Ralston about more character magazines," Gibson explained. "And I was thinking myself of a magician detective, though I didn't know how it would go. He said, 'Well, it's costly to start a character magazine, and if it flops....' So I suggested that they put out one with three characters in it. And then whichever one went well, that would be it. They went ahead, but they put in five or six characters. Everyone else used his own name, even Lester Dent with his Bufa stories, but they asked me if I would put on the 'Maxwell Grant' because then

they would advertise it in the Shadow magazine—'Get the stories by Maxwell Grant'—so it was really a favor to them on my part."

Nanovic recalled it this way:

"That was mostly my idea," he said. "And I don't want to brag about it because it didn't do too well. It just got along. Here we had a stable of famous writers. Gibson. Robeson. All of them were selling pretty well. So I said, 'The guys who like these fellas should like them in other magazines.' So we made up *Crime Busters*. These were all lead house names. We had like ten in every issue."

Henry W. Ralston and editor Nanovic ultimately decided to run more, shorter tales in what they dubbed *Crime Busters*. Gibson already had a character in mind, a traveling magician-sleuth named Norgil, which he wrote under the house name of Maxwell Grant. Ted Tinsley was contacted and created Carrie Cashin, a strong female detective. He did this under his own name.

No doubt Lester Dent was high on the list of writers S&S recruited for *Crime Busters*. His Doc Savage novels had been popular for four years. No doubt also, S&S attempted to prevail upon Dent to write the new series under the Kenneth Robeson house name. There is no doubt Dent resisted strenuously. He hated the Robeson byline, was initially surprised when the name was attached to his early Doc novels. Dent stood firm. He would contribute to the new magazine as Dent, or not at all.

Dent was a formula writer. He also loved gadgets. And by 1937 had developed a kind of screwball humor approach to Doc Savage.

From the little we know about it, a lot can be inferred about the genesis of Click Rush, the Gadget Man.

Sometime in 1936 but no later than June, 1937, Lester Dent rolled a carbon-paper sandwich into his Remington typewriter and rattled off the following:

TALKING DOG

The block of stone was about five feet long, two feet wide, and a foot thick. It was granite. It probably weighed over a ton.

It fell fifteen stories and missed John Magic by the length of an arm.

There was a crash. A hole burst open in the sidewalk, dust puffed and pieces of rock flew about, and across the street a man let out a yell. Or bleat.

Whether Dent changed his mind in mid-stride, or kept writing is unknown. Only this variant first page survived among his manuscripts.

During Dent's 1936 sabbatical from writing Doc Savage, he cracked several prestigious markets, including *Argosy* and *Black Mask*. He tried but failed to break into *Detective Fiction Weekly*. There is an excellent chance that the unpublished "Talking Dog" was a *DFW* reject that Dent dusted off when the *Crime Busters* opportunity arose.

It's possible Dent took the first adventure featuring John Magic into John Nanovic's office and got into a disagreement over the appropriate byline.

Whatever the case, in mid-June of 1937, Dent submitted "Talking Toad," the first adventure of Clickell Rush, the Gadget Man.

If the subject of the Kenneth Robeson byline came up that this point, Dent was prepared to hold his ground with Nanovic. Back in 1930, he had penned a novel featuring a San Francisco reporter named Click Rush. "The Thirteen Million Dollar Robbery" appeared in S&S's *The Popular*

Magazine. A sequel, "The Phantom Lagoon," was rejected and the manuscript since been lost. Since it was his character, Click Rush's new adventures would carry Dent's name. Lester had not forgotten his surprise and disappointment when his first Doc Savage novel was published under the short-lived house name of Kenneth Roberts. No one had told him in advance.

Whether or not this Click Rush is precisely the same character is open to question. There's not enough description and background in the 1930 novel to definitely say one way or another. The chief difference was that the Click Rush who battled through "The Thirteen Million Dollar Robbery" and its unpublished sequel was a true pulp hero.

Nanovic remembered Dent telling him he'd used the character before.

> "He did do those stories for somebody else before—I think," Nanovic related. "See, he wrote a lot of stuff. I think this was a character he wrote before and picked it up and put in here. He didn't do many of them, one or two."

Whatever the case, Dent stuck to his guns——and his true byline.

"Talking Toad" lead off the first issue of the new title, November 1937. (An excerpt had run in the last issue of *Best Detective,* the magazine *Crime Busters* replaced.) Included in Volume 1 Number 1 was coupon to entice reader reaction to the new set of characters.

Response was enthusiastic. Gadget Man was consistently one of the top reader favorites, with Norgil the magician and Carrie Cashin following a close second. Ironically, Norgil came in third. With these results in, Nanovic ordered his writers to expand the lengths of their stories, and this oddball trio became the spine of *Crime Busters*.

The premise of the Gadget Man seems to be a screwball variation on the original screwball detective, Nick Charles, hero of Dashiell Hammett's popular novel, *The Thin Man*. Rex Stout's Nero Wolfe novels—which Dent also read and admired—might have also supplied some inspiration. The mysterious Bufa was Wolfe, with poor Click Rush an unwilling Archie Goodwin.

The reincarnated Rush was a reluctant hero.

Gadget detectives had been a Dent staple since his 1932 *Detective-Dragnet* series about scientific criminologist Lynn Lash. A year later, there was Lee Nace, known as the "Blond Adder," in *Ten Detective Aces*. And in 1934, Foster Fade, the Crime Spectacularist, ran briefly in Dell's *All-Detective Magazine*.

Where did Dent get this idea? Well, his mother was a great gadgeteer, capable of building crystal radios and electrical chicken-coop warmers. Dent's lifelong love of tools and gadgets stemmed from her mechanically-inclined influence.

In literary terms, inspiration can be split between Arthur B. Reeve's pioneering scientific sleuth, Craig Kennedy, and Erle Stanley Gardner whose pulp heroes often relied on simple tricks like teargas fountain pens and the like.

Headquartered in the Imperial Apartments in Manhattan's Central Park West—where Dent lived on and off during the 1930s—Click Rush roamed around the country solving crimes with gadgets and electrical devices right out of Doc Savage.

Rush had no interest in solving crimes. He was an inventor. His life goal was to sell his crook-catching gadgets to police agencies, and thereby grow prosperous. Enter Bufa.

One day Rush discovers large papier-mâché toad in his

room. It comes with instructions to plug it in and insert a light bulb into its gaping mouth. Turns out it's a radio receiver that operates through city electrical wiring. The toad starts speaking:

> *"Hello,"* the toad said. *"You are, I presume, Mr. Rush?"*
>
> Rush frowned and leaned close to the toad. "Of all the damned fool things, this mess takes the prize. Someone is crazy. Nuts."
>
> *"I am Bufa,"* said the toad, *"of the species* Bufonidæ, *which feeds upon snails, slugs, insects, and such undesirable things."*
>
> *"Bufonidæ,"* Rush growled, "is the scientific name for the toad species. What has that got to do with this insane mess?"
>
> *"I am Bufa. I feed on snails, slugs, et cetera—of the human variety."*
>
> "Sure," Rush said. "That's all right. I suppose the keepers from whatever bughouse you got out of will find you eventually."
>
> *"You don't have much imagination, do you?"*
>
> "If it takes imagination to make this seem sensible, I'm all out to-day."
>
> There was no way, Rush thought, of locating the other person. Direction-finders would not locate a wired-wireless transmitter.
>
> *"For a long time,"* said the voice, *"I have been thinking of doing something like this."*
>
> "Like what?"
>
> *"Hiring an expert private detective to investigate crimes which I think need solving."*

Half of a ten-thousand dollar bill comes with the toad. Solve the mystery of the stainless steel frogs and the other half will come in the mail. Which a reluctant Rush proceeds to do.

For 18 hilarious episodes, Bufa bribes, bamboozles and otherwise bullies Rush into being his risk-taking legman. For his part, Rush vows to track down and unmask his disembodied tormentor. Their dysfunctional relationship drives the series.

When not succumbing to greed, Rush attempts to ditch the toad in various ways. Always, Bufa locates him. And the shenanigans begin anew. This combination of hard-boiled and screwball storytelling has acquired a modern appellation: "screwboiled."

The man shown examining a dummy head on the illustration heading the second story, "Death in Boxes," bears a striking and suspicious resemblance to Lester Dent himself. I doubt that is a coincidence.

The third adventure is typical. "Funny Faces" begins with the arresting first-line hook: "The man who was collecting noses had no nose himself." And so the faceless Bufa cajoles Rush into investigating a noseless man who had a mania for cutting off snoots of those who did.

The fifth exploit, "Windjam," was set in Dent's Miami dockside haunts where he used to sail. One of the best of this series, it was a salvage job. A story featuring a nautical detective named Cyrus Peace, a rustic corncob-smoking character who operated Admiralty Investigations in Miami, was rejected by *Detective Fiction Weekly*. So Dent converted it into a Click Rush story. Successfully, I might add.

This story was set around Pier No. 4, where Dent's *Black Mask* detective, Oscar Sail, anchored his sloop, and where Dent's *Albatross* spent winters.

"Les was very familiar with that spot," Norma Dent recalled. "Our boat was tied there for two winters. The boat next to ours was a cabin cruiser, owned by the Winchells, (Stewart Sterling) another well-known writer. However, he spent very little time on board his boat. Most of the time he lived in New York."

The *Four Winds* was another vessel anchored nearby. During the 1935 St. Petersburg-to-Havana boat race, Dent crewed on the 47-foot ketch, and spent six long days becalmed in the Gulf of Mexico. No doubt the *Four Winds* was the inspiration for the similarly-named *Fourth Wind* in "Windjam."

The *Albatross* spent her summers at New York's City Island, which is visited in "The Green Birds."

For some reason, toads and frogs keep popping up, as in "The Remarkable Zeke," where the recipient of a package discovers it contains a bullfrog, which he promptly stomps to death. On that thin thread, Dent hangs an entertaining tale.

All went swimmingly for two years. When Dent went to Europe, he took a vacation from Doc Savage. But he kept grinding out Click Rush tales. "The Itching Men" and "The Devils Smelled Nice" were written in Paris, and "Six White Horses," later reprinted in the 1942 *Detective Story Annual,* was inspired by Dent's 1938 European trip. One funny story, "The Monks and the Weasels," was set in LaPlata Missouri, where Dent was born, and where he lived during the final two decades of his life.

But S&S still wanted the Robeson name to appear in *Crime Busters.* So they prevailed on Dent to pen a similar series about an ex-prize fighter and reluctant detective named Ed Stone. Despite the famous byline, readers didn't take to Stone the way they had to Rush. After only seven adventures, Nanovic ordered Dent to concentrate on Click Rush exclusively. Ed Stone wasn't "clicking," according to Nanovic.

Probably Lester Dent would have continued pounding out Gadget Man novelettes long past the period where *Crime Busters* was retitled *Mystery Magazine* in 1939, but John Nanovic made an unfortunate mistake. He slapped the Kenneth Robeson byline on "The Frightened Yachtsman."

When the story appeared in the September, 1939 Crime Busters, Dent fired off a letter to Nanovic:

> "In reading the current issue of *Crime Busters,* I noticed that the house name, Kenneth Robeson, got on one of the Click Rush yarns. I hope this is an error, because I expended considerable effort in creating the character, and I cannot consent to it appearing under any name other than my own."

Nanovic shot back that the error was actually Dent's. An Ed Stone story had been promised by Dent, but Lester submitted a Click Rush instead. In making up the cover to that issue—covers were always printed before pulp interiors—Nanovic, in his own words, "figured the best way out was to use the name Robeson on it and cross my fingers. We had no comments on it, one way or another. The next Gadget yarn, however, continues under the name of Lester Dent, just as before. That happened to be one of those things."

Nanovic guessed wrong. Very wrong. Readers may not have cared, but Lester Dent did. There was no more correspondence about the matter after that. But the one remaining Gadget Man story on hand ran in *Mystery,* December, 1939. After that there were no more.

One has to assume that Dent was so peeved at the masking of his own byline, he simply stopped writing Gadget Man. There was also a change in buying policy at that point, which would limit a writer's resale options on his own stories, and this new restriction could have played a significant role as well.

If so, this was a terrible tragedy. For this was one of the great screwboiled characters of the pulps. While Dent teased the reader with the true identity of the man behind Bufa, the ubiquitous Talking Toad, he never gave any concrete hints, not even when Rush races to Los Angeles to track down Bufa through the Continental Detective Agency—Dent's nod to his all-time favorite detective writer, Dashiell Hammett, whose nameless Continental Op worked out of their San Francisco office—and comes as close as he ever did to unmasking his tormentor. This took place in "Run, Actor, Run!" and its sequel, "A Man and a Mess."

Ironically, decades after both men had died, Hammett's daughter revealed that her father was a regular reader of *Doc Savage Magazine!* Lester would have been astounded to know that—and no doubt proud.

Alas, we'll never read the Cuban adventure promised at the end of "The Green Birds."

Nor will we ever read a satisfactory conclusion to the series. Readers have speculated that Bufa was Doc Savage or one of is aides, such as electrical wizard Long Tom Roberts. But Dent would never have mixed a series of his own with one owned by S&S, so such speculation is completely out. It's tempting to suggest that this is the philanthropic hero of his *Argosy* serial, Genius Jones. Both Jones and Bufa have a penchant for elliptical speech. Both were created around the same time.

The longest series Lester Dent ever penned, sadly the Gadget Man stories have been neglected for years. And rarely reprinted. Happily, we are changing that lamentable oversight. Additionally, we have gone back to Lester

Dent's surviving carbons and restored missing text from every story that suffered editorial cuts for space and other reasons.

In 1940, artist Jack Farr adapted three of Dent's stories for Street & Smith's *Shadow Comics* and *Doc Savage Comics*. The strip was called "The Talking Toad" and Farr probably scripted them himself. Lester Dent never received credit for the feature and I suspect that it stopped after three installments because he complained about it.

As Dent's friend and fellow Street & Smith contributor Frank Gruber once said, "The Gadget Man stories were fantastic and showed a talent for invention that has not been surpassed by any other writer. Harry Stephen Keeler, perhaps, came closest but Lester Dent got as many fantastic tricks in a short story as Harry got in a complete novel."

So who was Bufa? Maybe you reading these fascinating stories can glean a clue from the adventures as they unfold....

—Will Murray

TALKING TOAD

BUFA, WHICH FEEDS ON SLUGS, SNAILS
AND INSECTS—HUMAN VARIETY!

CHAPTER 1

THE TOAD

THE BLOCK OF stone was about five feet long, two feet wide, and a foot thick. It was granite. It probably weighed over a ton.

It fell fifteen stories and missed Clickell Rush by the length of an arm.

There was a crash. A hole burst open in the sidewalk, dust puffed and pieces of rock flew about, and across the street a man let out a yell. Or bleat.

"Click" Rush looked up at fifteen stories of office building front and a nick in the top where the rock had been. Then Rush looked across the street.

The man who had bleated was a small, mild-looking sheep of a man in gray clothes. He was standing very still on the sidewalk with both hands over his mouth, like a woman who had just seen a kettle boil over on her new stove.

"See anything queer?" Rush called.

The sheep of a man just stood there.

Click Rush walked into the building, got into the elevator and rode upward and the operator stopped at the seventh floor of his own accord. There was no one else in the elevator, and no one had rung for seven. The operator waited expectantly, then looked at Rush and said, "Well?"

"The top floor was where I started for," Rush said.

"Oh." The operator rolled the doors shut and moved the control handle to *up*. "They got an agency on seven," he explained. "Gets jobs for acrobats. I kinda figured from your looks that you might be one of them acrobats." The operator watched floor numbers streak past.

Click Rush did not say anything. He got out on the top floor, climbed a naked concrete stairs. He was not a large man, and not small, either. He had a wiry, trained look, and a frame that carried no spare flesh anywhere. He had the appearance of a man who had trained too hard, or who had worked too hard for too long a time at something. His suit was business brown, his eyes brown, his hair brown, and the watch on his right wrist had a brown band. His mouth was too large.

He stepped out on a black-tarred roof top where black soot flakes traveled around slowly.

At once, he saw a grimy gunny sack at his feet. He kicked the sack, and it rattled; he kicked it again, and a short steel crowbar showed.

There was a film of soot on the tarred roof. In the film, a long smear, and when Rush got down and got the sun right, he saw plainly that the smear led to the gap in the roof coping where the rock had been. Someone had walked to the coping and back, using the gunny sack like a mop on the end of the crowbar to wipe out footprints.

Rush went over to the coping and saw the marks where the crowbar had pried loose the rock.

He looked over the edge for some time. There was a crowd on the sidewalk, but no sign of the mild-looking little man who had been so horrified.

Rush went downstairs and stared at the crowd. Still he saw no sign of the mild man.

Rush bought a newspaper, walked to the corner, got on the subway, hung to one of the white-painted hand straps and manipulated the newspaper with one hand.

He had read the newspaper story once before, but he was wondering if he could have overlooked something that would explain why somebody, for some unknown reason, had tried to kill him by prying a rock off the roof edge. He was puzzled. He had no enemies. He knew no more than half a dozen people in New York City, none intimately.

CLICKELL RUSH'S picture was on the second page of the newspaper. Below the picture, it said:

> Crime Super-scientist and one of his thousand inventions. The box contains a device which will show whether you are innocent or guilty from the kind of fingerprint you make.

The box which Rush held in the picture was black and about

the size of a shoe box. There was a story with the picture, too. The story read:

COPS CAN'T SEE SUPER-SCIENTIST— JUST A BUG

Clickell Rush, who came to the city with the notion of selling super-modern, crook-catching gadgets to the police—didn't.

Rush is a serious-looking young man with the build of a professional athlete, who says he lived as a hermit for several years while he invented over a thousand gadgets to catch crooks.

Police Commissioner Michaels said, "I advised this Rush to devote his talents to inventing a machine to go to Mars, or somewhere."

THERE WAS more of the story, mostly wisecracks by Police Commissioner Michaels, who was positive the city's police department had no need of trick gadgets.

Rush still saw nothing in the story to explain why anyone should try to smash him with a rock.

He grew aware that a man hanging to the next strap in the subway train was reading the paper. The man seemed intensely interested. His eyebrows and lower lip stuck out, but the rest of his face was mostly flat. He was a thick man. His lips moved as he read.

Rush handed him the newspaper. "Maybe you can figure it out," Rush said.

"Huh? What? I beg your pardon!"

"It does seem kind of crazy," Rush remarked. "Yes, but it couldn't very well be anything else. Someone read that and decided to drop rocks."

"I—wush—huh—" The thick man swallowed and sidled away.

"Er—my paper, if you don't mind," Rush said, and recovered the newspaper.

He killed about twenty puzzled minutes eating breakfast in a cafeteria.

CLICK RUSH saw that someone had been in his office. The match he had stuck in the crack at the top of the door, between the door and the frame, had fallen out. It lay on the old office-building floor. The match would not have fallen out had some one not opened the door.

The office was one Rush had rented for the purpose of demonstrating his gadgets to the police. He had fixed it up for that object. The police hadn't been interested enough to let him demonstrate.

He knew by now that he should have made his approach to the police through someone known to them, not directly. He had gone to them cold, and they had thought he was a nut. He could see why. Some of the gadgets he had perfected did sound fantastic.

Out of the right-side pocket of his coat—the coat was good, if worn—Rush took a pack of cigarettes.

He never smoked.

He put a match to the cigarette, puffed it to get it burning, then walked into his room. He looked around—the outer room, the inner room, behind a secondhand divan which he had bought, along with some chairs, a desk, a table to fit the place up. Then he looked in the washroom.

He stood in the washroom door and frowned at the man lying on the floor, a knife in his chest.

Then he put the cigarette out before the heat got to the chemical which, when burned, became tear gas.

He went back into the outer office and looked at the toad.

It wasn't a real toad. No toad was ever that big. A foot and a half long, a foot high. The thing was greenish-brown on the back, Missouri River-yellow on the belly, had a few warts, the eyes of a tomcat, and an open mouth red enough to have lately held raw meat. It sat on the table and looked hungry.

Under the paper was one half of the largest denomination of bill which Uncle Sam prints. Ten thousand dollars.

On the paper was one line printed with a typewriter. It read:

Put a lighted electric light bulb in the toad's mouth.

Click Rush frowned at the toad, the paper, and one half of ten thousand dollars. He rubbed his jaw. It was a hard jaw. The hand which rubbed it had sinews which stood out with movement.

"This," he said, "gets crazier."

He went to the washroom again.

The man was dead, of course. The knife blade was an inch wide, and from its location in the man's chest, probably passed through the geometric center of the victim's heart. There was not much red leakage on the washroom floor, for men do not bleed to any extent after they are dead. The heart stops pumping through the wound.

The dead one was the thick fellow who had read the newspaper over Rush's shoulder in the subway.

Rush sank to a knee and examined the soles of the man's shoes. They did not look like American-made shoes, and Rush removed one of them.

The shoe had been made in China.

On the shoe sole was enough black soot and a bit of black tar roofing compound to show he had been on a roof. On his trouser legs, just above the knee, was a bit of mortar dust, the same color as that on the roof coping from which the rock had been pried.

There was a little fuzz from a gunny sack inside the man's coat, where he might have carried the sack.

The only thing in the dead man's pocket was a steamship ticket to Ireland.

CLICK RUSH withdrew from the washrooms, got out a handkerchief and blotted his forehead. His face had a sleepy look—a drowsy expression that came from intense concentration.

The thick man had tried to kill him; then, the man had been killed in Rush's office—concentration was not enough to figure that one out.

Rush went to a trunk—half a dozen large wardrobe trunks stood in the outer office—and opened it. The trunk was marked "No. 1." He removed a portable device from the trunk. The contrivance was a portable X-ray, with various uses, including the examining of the contents of strange packages.

After he had X-rayed the toad from various angles, he was convinced that its viscera did not comprise anything in the nature of nitroglycerin. He remembered the note's instructions:

"Put a lighted electric light bulb in the toad's mouth."

He followed them out, unscrewing an electric bulb from a floor stand so he could get the shade off, screwing the bulb back in, turning it on, and inserting it in the toad's gaping red mouth. It was a forty-watt bulb.

By pressing an ear to the toad's head, he heard the faint click of a thermostat as it was closed by warmth from the light bulb. Then there was a hum, and Rush, placing finger tips against the toad's stomach, felt vibration.

He knew then that the interior of the toad consisted of a wired radio "transceiver," a device which would take high-frequency waves off the electric light wires as an ordinary radio takes them out of the air.

"Uh—hello," he said to the toad.

"Hello," the toad said. *"You are, I presume, Mr. Rush?"*

Rush frowned and leaned close to the toad. "Of all the damned fool things, this mess takes the prize. Someone is crazy. Nuts."

"I am Bufa," said the toad, *"of the species* Bufonidæ, *which feeds upon snails, slugs, insects, and such undesirable things."*

"Bufonidæ," Rush growled, "is the scientific name for the toad species. What has that got to do with this insane mess?"

"I am Bufa. I feed on snails, slugs, et cetera—of the human variety."

"Sure," Rush said. "That's all right. I suppose the keepers from whatever bughouse you got out of will find you eventually."

"You don't have much imagination, do you?"

"If it takes imagination to make this seem sensible, I'm all out to-day."

There was no way, Rush thought, of locating the other person. Direction-finders would not locate a wired wireless transmitter.

"For a long time," said the voice, *"I have been thinking of doing something like this."*

"Like what?"

"Hiring an expert private detective to investigate crimes which I think need solving."

"I'm not an expert private detective," Rush growled.

"You're not?"

"No!"

"You don't want to work for me?" asked the voice.

"I do not."

"Wouldn't the other half of that ten-thousand-dollar bill interest you?"

Rush snorted. "The other half of that bill would interest anybody."

"Good. Solve this crime and you get it."

"You mean," Rush snapped, "solve the murder of this man dead in my washroom?"

"What? What?"

"And solve why he tried to kill me with a rock?"

"Kill you! What on earth are you talking about?"

Rush said, "If I solve anything, it'll be the mystery of who you are. My idea is that you are somebody who should be in a straitjacket."

The toad purred in silence for some moments. Evidently the other was thinking.

"At six o'clock, put the electric light in Bufa's mouth again," the voice said. *"I'll be anxious to learn how you are getting along."*

"I'm not," Rush said, "taking any job from a crazy man."

"I assure you I am not unbalanced."

"They never think they are."

The toad sighed.

"You might," it said, *"read about the stolen frogs in the newspaper."*

That was all the toad had to say.

CHAPTER II

AGGRAVATING WOMAN

RUSH STARED AT the thing, took off his hat, ran fingers through his hair, and his mouth warped around into various puzzled shapes. He backed away from the toad, still eyeing it, and took out his handkerchief again to mop his forehead. He laughed. It was a laugh that sounded like something dropped, and he seemed startled by it, for his face straightened, and he sat down in one of the chairs and remained there for a time.

Then he got up and looked through the newspaper again. He found something he had missed before. He read:

FROGS STOLEN

Police were called yesterday to investigate the disappearance of a shipment of stainless-steel frogs which were stolen from a warehouse.

The frogs, one thousand in number, were being shipped from Shanghai, China, to a man named Pat O'Reilly, of Dublin, Ireland. The stainless-steel frogs were in the warehouse awaiting transshipment to a steamer bound for Ireland.

There was nothing else in the paper about frogs, stainless steel or otherwise. He threw the paper away.

The toad was not hard to dissect. Rush wore rubber gloves to do the job, leaving no fingerprints. The mechanism, the parts, tubes, coils, and so on were ordinary and could be bought at too many places to have much hope of tracing the builder of the toad from that source.

He tested for fingerprints with iodine vapor processes. There were plenty of fingerprints. It took him half an hour to decide they had all been made by one man, and the prints were deep enough in the toad's mechanism to convince him the man who made the prints had built the "transceiver."

The builder of the toad had a right hand with a middle finger that for some reason or other left no fingerprints.

There were other things which Rush could tell generally from the prints. The man was probably white, middle-aged and had small hands. The fact that the middle finger of the right hand left no prints was the most interesting, though.

When knuckles tapped the door, Rush lighted another cigarette, and opened it. He put out the cigarette at once.

The stranger was a smallish kind of a girl, about twenty, and brownish. There was a healthy look to her, the brown coming from health and sun and not from her race—she was American, Rush thought, and rather sweet to look at. Still, the way they looked didn't always mean what it seemed.

"Hello," she said. "Invite me in, will you?"

"Come in," Rush said.

She took a step inside, and instantly, he looked for the thing that made her walk that way—short and unbalanced and unsteady.

Her feet—

She had bound feet. Not bound with ropes. They weren't bound at all, but shod in delicate pumps. But they looked as though they had been bound in her youth, after the Chinese fashion with their women. They were tiny, hardly larger than her fists. But she didn't look Chinese.

"Sure, and it's glad I am to find you," she said.

Irish, he thought. Right from County Cork.

"I'm glad, too," Rush said dryly. "Glad to find something that looks sensible."

She studied him. A corner of her mouth moved slightly.

"Something more sensible," she suggested, "than stainless-steel frogs."

He nodded.

"And falling rocks," he added. "And a talking toad named Bufa, and half a ten-thousand-dollar bill, and a dead man in my washroom."

"Dead—"

She didn't get out through the door. Rush, jumping, planted himself in front of her, and reaching behind him, locked the door.

"Yes," Rush said. "It is startling, at that."

She was scared. Her hands shook a little.

"Dead man—talking toad—falling rock—a ten-thousand-dollar bill—" She looked terrified.

"Only half of the bill," Rush said seriously. "That's the hell of it. Only half of ten thousand dollars."

"Are you—crazy?" she asked uncertainly.

"That," Rush said, "has occurred to me."

SHE TOOK a step away from him, and so poor was her balance on her feet that she stumbled. He stepped forward to help her remain erect but she squeaked—rather than screamed—and whipped away, lost her balance completely and fell into an overstuffed chair.

"I can't think of anything more aggravating," Rush said, "than half of ten thousand dollars, without the other half."

The girl stared at him wordlessly.

Rush went around to a trunk, opened it, fumbled inside, turning knobs. Then he took a package of cigarettes out of the trunk, as though that was what he had been after.

"Smoke?" he asked.

She only stared.

"Of course," Rush said, "there's the frogs. They're made of stainless steel. They were being shipped to a man named O'Reilly, in Ireland. By the way, do you know Mr. O'Reilly?"

The girl turned pale.

"Do you know O'Reilly?" Rush repeated.

The girl got whiter. She looked as though she were going to faint.

"I believe you do know O'Reilly," Rush said.

He stepped forward suddenly, grasped the girl before she could arise, almost carried her to the washroom door, and showed her the dead man there. He felt her tighten, every muscle of her, in his arms.

Carrying her back, he put her in the inner office, where she sprawled limp and tight-lipped.

"Was that O'Reilly?" he asked.

She seemed speechless.

"Is the dead man O'Reilly?" Rush repeated.

She swallowed as if she were trying to get something big out of the way.

"It's Bent," she said. "Bent—"

"And who is Bent?"

"O'Reilly's aide-de-camp," she said in a low voice.

"What does O'Reilly look like?"

She seemed to be recovering from shock. "O'Reilly is a small, peaceful-looking man," she said.

Then the girl looked down at her feet. She leaned over and stared at them. Her hands fastened tightly to the arms of the old chair, and the fingertips dug in. Her mouth drew back at the corners, and her whole face changed, as if she wanted to scream out in awful horror.

"O'Reilly is the worst devil who ever lived!" she cried shrilly. She began screaming: "He's a fiend! He's a butcherer! He's never had but one man, never known but one man, who didn't want to kill him. And that man was Bent, who is dead in there!"

Rush waited. She did not say anything more.

"Just why," Rush asked, "did you come here?"

She stared at him. She seemed to go far back in her mind and capture something that had been scared away.

"I wanted," she said, "to show you where you can find the stainless-steel frogs."

"You—*hm-m-m.*"

She stood up suddenly, balancing herself with a hand on the chair. "We'd better go."

"You mean after the frogs?"

"Yes."

Remembering the fellow who had clapped his hands over his mouth just after the rock fell from the coping, Rush looked at her thoughtfully. "O'Reilly is a little sheep of a man," he said.

"Yes," the girl said, and stiffened.

"The middle finger of his right hand is not, by any chance, missing?"

"No," she said.

"Who has the missing finger?"

She shook her head. "No one that I know of."

"The finger might be bandaged," Rush said.

"You must mean Henry Hay," she said. "Do you mean Hay?"

"Maybe I do. Who is he?"

"A friend of O'Reilly," the girl said.

"Thought you said O'Reilly didn't have any friends?"

"He hasn't. Henry Hay used to work for him in China."

"What doing?"

"I'm not going to tell you anything more."

"What did O'Reilly and Henry Hay do in China?" Rush repeated.

"I'm not saying more. I do not understand this at all."

"I don't get it either," Rush said. "It kind of aggravates me." He walked over to the girl. "Have you got a name?"

"June," she said. "June David."

"It aggravates me, June," Rush said. "But none of it aggravates me quite as much as you do."

He picked her up, and she kicked and struck, dug at his eyes, pulled his hair, but did not prevent his carrying her to the inner office, dropping her into a chair, and leaving her locked in the room.

BACK IN the outer office, he went to the trunk from which he had taken the cigarettes earlier. He examined the lie detector which he had turned on while pretending to get the cigarettes. The detector measured changes in the micro-currents of a human body, and its antenna was concealed in the chair which the girl had coupled. He had rigged the device up to demonstrate to the police.

According to the lie detector, the girl had told the truth about everything except the reason for her visit. She had lied when she said she had come to show him the whereabouts of the stainless-steel frogs.

He was eyeing the graph of the detector when there was a faint whirring sound from another trunk. He opened it, and watched another device. A tape moved slowly, and on this, a stylus was inking dashes.

The stylus inked four dashes, one dash, then six, eight, seven, three, three dashes.

The gadget was a pickup for long distance eavesdropping on telephone lines. The dashes were the recording of a number being dialed. DA 6-733 was probably the number, Rush decided. The DA exchange would be Dartmouth, which was the only DA exchange.

He picked up the telephone receiver attached to the device.

"Yes," he heard a deep voice say.

"Dad... Dad, he didn't fall for it!" the girl gasped. "We can't decoy him someplace, grab him and hold him until the thing quiets down."

"Oh, we won't give up yet," said the man's voice. "We can try another gag on him."

"I'm afraid of him," the girl said quickly. "Apparently he has no nerves at all. And he knows more than we thought he did. He knows something of O'Reilly, and he knows about Henry Hay. He even knows Hay has a bandaged forefinger on his right hand."

"But he's never seen Hay."

"That—I thought that, too."

"Just how much does he know?"

"I—I'm not sure."

"Well, I wouldn't worry too much. I just figured we'd better get him out of the way." The deep male voice made a disgusted sound. "I'd like to know who that was telephoned us and said this fellow Rush was investigating the stolen frogs business."

"You still haven't found out who called?"

"How could we? It was just a voice. I never heard it before."

"You are certain it wasn't O'Reilly?"

"Positive." The man snorted. "O'Reilly doesn't know anything about us, or about this Rush being mixed up in it."

"Bent is dead here in Rush's office."

"Bent is... what? Dead? Bent?"

"Here in the office of this Crime Super-scientist, as the newspapers called him." The girl's voice held shrill terror.

"But.... Great grief! How—who killed him?"

"I don't know. This Rush might have. I don't think he did, though. I—I don't know who killed Bent."

There was silence.

"You'd better get away from there," the man said.

"All right."

"You're not in trouble, June?"

"No," the girl said instantly. "I'm in a drugstore."

That ended the conversation.

CHAPTER III

MILD LITTLE MAN

"**YOU'RE QUITE A** liar, aren't you?" Rush asked the girl.

She looked at him blankly. "I don't understand you."

"Never mind." He frowned at her thoughtfully. "By the way, a man telephoned you and told you and your father I was interested in stainless-steel frogs, so you thought you'd—er—restrain me for a while—"

"How—" She popped her eyes at him.

"What I want to know," Rush continued, "is this: Did the man who telephoned you call himself Bufa, by any chance?"

"I—how did you know that?"

"It was Bufa, then?"

"He said"—the girl stared steadily—"that he was Bufa of the species something-or-other which fed on slugs, insects and things. We—it was crazy."

"Same guy," Rush said.

"Same—this doesn't make sense!"

"It makes just a little bit more than it did," Rush said. "I think we might go look at the stainless-steel frogs now, if you don't mind."

"I—that is— Well, all right." The girl was almost incoherent.

They went out into the hall and to the elevator, and

Rush offered his arm, and the girl took it, for she really needed help in walking. Rush helped the girl inside. Then he snapped a finger.

"Forgot something!" he exclaimed. "Hold the cage a minute, huh?"

"Sure," said the operator.

Rush walked away. He did not go to his office, but ducked into the stairway, and began descending with long leaps. It was many flights, and by the time he reached the bottom, he had acquired a method, by sliding hands on the railing for balance and jumping, whereby he could take half a flight with each jump.

He ran out through the lobby, looked up and down the street, then got in a taxicab across the street, ignoring one that was parked directly in front of the building.

"Hold it a minute," he said.

It was not a minute. It was hardly more than twenty seconds before the girt came out of the building, running, using her arms to balance herself on her strange feet, and got in the convenient cab. She had persuaded the operator to bring her down, evidently.

"Follow that yellow," Rush told his driver.

The girl's yellow cab moved slowly, took the first corner north, and went a little faster.

"Don't lose it," Rush warned.

"Keep your shirt on, pal," requested the driver.

A department-of-sanitation man was washing down the street with a fire hose, and the water slopped briefly against the cab, filled the interior with dusty smelling spray, for an instant. The driver said something profane about his wash job on the hack, ending with, "If it ain't one damn thing, it's two others."

Click Rush remained silent, kept his eyes on the girl's machine.

When she got out of her cab, it was in front of a raw-looking building that might have been a slab of upended brick street with windows inset, then scabbed over with boards. She ran up steps to a door that needed painting, and passed through the doorway.

"Next corner," Rush told his driver.

He got out, paid the man, and found there was an alley; then, he went down this to the old building which the girl had entered. The back door was not, he discovered, locked, and he pushed it and it opened. Then he listened, but heard no sound, and entered. The search he conducted was slow at first, and cautious, then more speedy and disgusted. There were three floors of gloom, litter, rat smell, dropped plaster and creaking boards, and a roof top which needed repairs. But no girl.

"Nice trick," Rush grumbled.

THERE WERE two telephone booths in the cigar store two blocks away, and one was out of order. Rush said into the instrument in the other: "Sergeant McGoosey of the police homicide squad wants to know the address of the telephone with the number Dartmouth 6-8733."

"You say Sergeant McGoosey of the police?" the operator asked.

"There's been a man murdered."

"Oh," said the operator. "Just a minute." There was a delay and Rush read the instructions, on a card above the telephone, about how to get a policeman, a fireman or an ambulance. "It's at 112 North Davis Street," the operator said.

"Thank you very much."

North Davis Street was in a residential suburb—four dollars and eighty cents' worth from the business district, Rush observed, watching the taxicab meter gloomily. No. 112 was a large block of red brick sitting in a great nest of green shrubbery which was enclosed by a low, red brick wall. Rush directed the cab around to the other side of the block.

"Would you like to wait?" he asked.

"I'd like four-eighty better," said the driver, "on account of sometimes they don't come back."

"I hope," Rush said truthfully, "that you're not a clair-voyant."

"A what?"

"They see into the future, you know. They can tell when people aren't coming back."

"I've just had experience," the driver said.

Rush paid the four-eighty, which left him, he saw when he counted funds, less than a dollar in silver, and one end of a ten-thousand-dollar bill which was useless without the other end. "I don't think," he told the driver, "that you'd better wait."

The brick wall was low, the brush beyond thick and concealing, and there was, Rush found after scouting a bit, a side door convenient to the shrubbery, and a basement window.

The door was locked, so he took the window, which was open. He went in head-first, which is a quiet way to go into a basement window, and thus was able to lift aside a leaning broom which otherwise he would doubtless have kicked over, making a racket.

He waited. It was remarkably gloomy in the basement, and after his eyes became accustomed, he steered around a pingpong table to a stairway and went up, testing each tread with his hands. None of them squeaked. The door at the top did not squeak, and he found himself in a paneled hallway, with the white enamel of a kitchen at one end and various doors in the other direction.

Voices behind one of the doors drew him.

A strange man's voice was saying in a calm, conversational tone: "They're beautiful frogs, aren't they? Perfect specimens of their kind."

"They're good enough," the girl's voice said.

"Yes," agreed the voice of the man whom the girl had called by telephone from Rush's office. "At any rate, they do not look what they are."

There was a silence.

"Shall we retire to another room?" asked the first man.

Rush realized the speaker was the mild little fellow who had been across the street, who had clapped his hands over his mouth when the rock fell.

Feet stirred. They were leaving the room. Rush retreated quickly, but it was not necessary, because they did not come out in the hall. Instead, they left the room by another door.

After a moment, Rush entered the room where they had been.

It was a large room, bookcases around the walls, deep chairs, a desk, reading lamps, a radio. Furniture had been cleared to make a space in the center. In the space stood an array of packing cases, at least twenty of them, and the top had been knocked off every one.

The stainless-steel frogs had been lifted out of some. The excelsior packing was scattered. Rush picked up one of the frogs, casually, with one hand—and it slipped from his fingers, nearly fell before he caught it.

The frog was much heavier than he had expected.

HOLDING THE frogs with both hands, turning them, resting them on the wooden cases when his fingers began to ache from their weight, Rush examined them. They were solid metal, of course. And the workmanship was exquisite, apparently hand carving. The frogs were works of art.

They did not resemble the talking toad in anything but a general way.

The markings on the battered wooden shipping cases indicated the frogs had been shipped from Shanghai, China, and were destined for a Pat O'Reilly in Dublin, Ireland. That checked with the newspaper story about the stolen frogs, as they were evidently the same frogs.

He was looking in some of the remaining cases at more frogs when a voice spoke gently.

"Wonderful specimens, don't you think?" the voice inquired.

It was the gentle-looking little fellow who had stood across the street when the rock fell. He stood, mild as a sheep, just inside the door, smiling slightly.

"I—hello," Rush said.

"They're my frogs," said the small man pleasantly. "I am rather proud of them."

"They're nice-looking frogs, all right," Rush said dryly. "I take it you're Mr. O'Reilly?"

"O'Reilly—yes." He looked contrite. "I'm sorry they have caused you so much trouble. I do hope I can do something to repay you. Isn't there something I can do?"

"You might explain things," Rush said.

"Ah—what do you wish explained?"

"Practically all of it."

The little man smiled. "Won't you join us in the other room? The others will be glad to verify anything I tell you."

Rush nodded, and they went into another room, where the girl with the strangely small feet and a large leathery man with steely eyes and a scar on his left cheek, a nick in his right ear, sat in chairs—with their wrists and ankles bound with rope.

Rush wheeled. "What—"

The mild sheep of a man was holding a blue revolver.

"If this gun had a silencer," said he, "I'd kill you now. Sit down!"

Rush sat down.

"Do you mind if I smoke a cigarette?" he asked.

"I'm afraid," said O'Reilly, "that I'd mind almost anything you do except sit still."

THE SMALL, mild man sat down and watched Rush intently, holding his gun. He shook his head. "I think I shall play safe and make no attempt to tie you until my men come," he said.

"Your men?" Rush grunted.

The mild man smiled.

The girl volunteered, "O'Reilly has two men with him. He had three, but one, Bent, was killed."

"Killed by Henry Hay," O'Reilly added.

The girl added, "And now he's sent them to get Hay."

The small man shook his head. "I wouldn't talk any more," he advised.

The tone was mild, but there was something deadly in it. Rush fell to studying the fellow. He began to notice things he had missed before—fine scars, an ugly light in the mild eyes, a vicious cast to the mouth at times.

Convinced that O'Reilly would shoot if crossed, Rush remained quiet in the chair. The girl, June, and the leathery old man with the steely eyes—dad, she had called him over the telephone—hardly stirred. Rush, at first, thought they were not greatly concerned. Later, he knew they were. What he had mistaken for patience was intense strain.

Catching the girl's eyes, he formed, "What next?" silently with his lips.

With flinging abruptness, "He's going to kill all of us!" she said.

The small man sprang up. "If there's any more talking, I'll do it now!"

The girl's father snarled, "Now is as good as later!" and tried to come erect, but only managed to unbalance himself and fall heavily beside his chair.

O'Reilly showed even, white teeth.

"It's too bad I haven't got the facilities I had in China," he said.

"You damned fiend!" the leathery man gritted.

O'Reilly looked at him malevolently.

"Of course," he said, "your daughter hasn't any more toes to spare. But there are other things I could do."

The significance of that—what it might mean—soaked into Rush. He came up straight, tight. The small man grimaced, rather than smiled.

"Yes," he said. "It's what you think. Her father and I had a slight difficulty. A matter of how we were to divide up when we dissolved the partnership. Unfortunately, I had to show him his daughter's toes before he agreed to—er—my ideas."

Rush had thought the girl's feet had merely been bound in youth. But she had been tortured—

Something in Rush's reaction must have tickled the mild little man. He chuckled.

"It was really appropriate in China," he said. "You see, we were war lords."

"War—" Rush scowled. "Who's kidding who here?"

"War lord—it is the truth," O'Reilly said. "There are a number of military leaders in China who are not Chinese." He moved his gun slightly. "Quiet, please. I think my men are returning."

Three men came into the room.

CHAPTER IV

BUFA SPEAKS

TWO OF THE men carried guns, foreign automatics with long spike barrels. The third man was thin, gray-headed and quite remarkably freckled, and the middle finger of his right hand was bandaged.

"Henry Hay," Rush said suddenly.

The gray-headed man glanced up in answer to the name, but did not say anything.

"Say something," Rush said. "Where did they catch you, Hay?"

Rush wanted him to speak. Henry Hay's fingerprints had been inside the talking toad, so he had built the thing, but what Rush wanted to know was whether his voice would be that of the man who had spoken over the wired radio inside the toad.

But Henry Hay did not speak.

O'Reilly showed his teeth. "I'm glad to see you know Hay," he said grimly. "It seems that no one is trying to deceive anybody."

"I never saw him before," Rush said.

"The hell you didn't," snarled the mild man. "When my frogs were stolen, I went to Hay for help. Hay is a private detective, and I told him not to involve anybody else in the frog business. But he rang you in."

Hay spoke.

"I didn't!" he said.

Rush knew then that Hay was *not* the man who had spoken through the medium of the wired radio toad.

O'Reilly said, "I had my men trailing you. They heard you tell someone over the telephone that everything was set to put this Clickell Rush to work on the job."

Hay swallowed.

"Furthermore," said O'Reilly, "Bent followed you to this Rush's room, and you killed him."

"Self-defense!" Hay snapped.

"Of course," O'Reilly agreed. "I know it was. Bent had orders to kill you."

Rush stood up.

"Sit down!" O'Reilly shoved out his gun. To his men, he said, "I've been holding this bird. Search him for me, will you."

"Who is he?"

"Some kind of a detective with gadgets, the newspapers said."

ONE OF the men went through Rush's pockets, emptying the contents on a table—pack of cigarettes, matches, handkerchief, a small screw driver, the half of the ten-thousand-dollar bill. Nothing to arouse suspicion.

"Gleeps, ten grand!" exploded the searcher. "Where's the other half of this?" He shoved Rush. "Come on, where is it?"

Rush looked at Henry Hay. "Where is it?"

Hay swallowed. He was scared. "I don't know anything about it."

"That's funny. You left it in my office." Rush scowled.

"I mean," Hay groaned, "that I don't know who was behind that. I just got the toad and some money, a note and that half of a bill. The note said to leave the toad in your office with the half of a bill and instructions to put a light in the toad's mouth and turn it on."

O'Reilly didn't look so mild. "What is this? It's news to me. What is it?"

"I don't know anything," Henry Hay said, "except what I told you."

O'Reilly cocked his gun, said nothing.

Hay, terror-stricken, wailed, "I don't know, I tell you! I did find a microphone planted in my office. Maybe someone was eavesdropping. I don't know! I really—oh, please—you're not going to kill me—"

O'Reilly gestured at Rush. "Tie him up. We'll finish this."

Rush stirred. "I'd like a cigarette," he said.

"Tie him up," O'Reilly repeated.

O'Reilly eyed him narrowly. Then the mild man—he had only flashes of looking like an ex-Chinese war lord—moved over to Rush's cigarettes. He tore one of them apart and examined it, then made a startled noise and threw the stuff on the floor.

"Yeah," he said. "The solidified type of tear gas. Turns into vapor when you burn it."

Rush sighed, relaxed in his chair, and looked as defeated as he could.

"You win," he muttered. He swallowed. "But I'd like a cigarette anyway."

O'Reilly showed his teeth. He drew cigarettes from his own pocket, took one, put it between his lips and said, the paper cylinder bobbing, "Tie him up. Then gag them."

The men advanced on Rush.

O'Reilly reached over, got one of the matches which had been in Rush's pocket, and struck it.

There was a deafening report.

RUSH CAME out of the chair. He was set, ready. He had hoped the man would take one of the matches and fail to notice that it was a cleverly molded and colored chemical composition with the explosive power of trinitrotoluene.

O'Reilly was screaming. The girl was on the floor, rolling over and over for the door. Her father flopped like a fish out of water for O'Reilly.

Rush got the first man. Around the neck. The fellow struggled for his gun. Rush held the fellow's neck in the crook of his arm, squeezed, then let go. The man cursed, stumbled back, still trying to get his gun out; he did get it out, but something happened to him. He shook his head violently, batting his eyes, and his mouth opened, his knees hinged, and he sat down. He began to scream in a feeble, mad way, and seemed to go to sleep while still screaming.

Rush had hold of the second man by then. He got his arms around that one's chest. They wrestled and fell down.

Henry Hay and the girl's father, working together, upset O'Reilly.

Rush squeezed his man, and held on. He got kicked in the shins, bitten, and his head knocked on the floor. He still held on. A table upset, and a vase of flowers came down on them. Parts of the vase crunched under their struggling bodies. Then Rush's opponent began to scream, and his cries feebled, and he relaxed.

About that time, O'Reilly shot Henry Hay through the brain.

Rush lunged, grabbed O'Reilly, got the gun hand, and they fell on the girl's father and on the dying man; and the latter's kicking and threshing, like a chicken with its head off, tossed them about. Rush straightened his arm and brought it against O'Reilly time after time, striking as a snake strikes.

For the chemical-filled repeating hypodermic needle strapped to his upper arm, against the skin, discharged repeatedly into O'Reilly. The needle was covered with sponge rubber for two reasons—when the forearm was felt, its presence was not noticeable; and it would discharge only when a great deal of force was exerted, avoiding accidents.

O'Reilly collapsed.

Rush ran into the hallway, got the girl, and hauled her back into the room.

He gathered up the guns.

Then he went into the other room, came back with one of the frogs, and gave it several hard raps with the barrel of one of the guns. It seemed hard. He put it on the floor and fired at it. The bullet opened considerable of a groove in the frog, and Rush scratched in the groove with a gun sight.

"Hard on the outside, but softer inside," he said. "And none of the stuff is stainless steel." He looked at the girl. "Gold, isn't it? Mixed in an alloy with silver to make it white. And maybe alloyed with some other metals to make it harder."

She nodded.

"The frogs are gold," she said.

Rush said, "I'm going to call the police. Want to tell me any more before they get here?"

She hesitated.

"Go ahead," her father said.

"O'Reilly and my father were once partners in China, and O'Reilly robbed us." She shuddered. "That was when he—my feet—the fiend!"

"They'll electrocute him," Rush said. "What about the frogs?"

"O'Reilly fled from China—the government broke up his bandit army. The gold was his loot. He had it made into frogs, and shipped to himself in Ireland, his home. He intended to retire, I suppose. Anyway, we learned about it. We—we have friends in China. We hijacked the frogs here in New York, to get back what he took from us."

"That's not all," Rush said.

"It's all I know—someone—we don't know who—telephoned us that you were going to solve the case. That brought on—this."

"There's someone," Rush said sourly, "who hasn't appeared in this at all—in person."

"The man who called himself Bufa," offered the girl's father.

"Exactly."

Rush frowned at Henry Hay. "I have a suspicion that Hay knew who Bufa is."

"Hay is dead."

"I'll call the police," Rush said.

It was five o'clock that afternoon before the police decided to turn Rush loose.

SIX O'CLOCK.

Clickell Rush shooed the last reporter out of his small office suite, closed the door and locked it, then went to the floor lamp. As he had done that morning, he removed the shade and inserted the lighted bulb in the mouth of the ridiculous-looking toad disguise for a wired radio "transceiver." Waiting for the heat to turn the device on, via the thermostat, he discovered he was holding his breath. If, after all, Henry Hay had been Bufa, this would be the end. And, among other things, the whereabouts of the other end of the bill now back in his pocket might remain a mystery—

The "transceiver" speaker began to hum.

"Ah—hello," Rush said tentatively.

The toad chuckled.

"I believe," it said, *"that I made a good choice. I have been reading, the newspapers."*

"It's all over, if that's what you mean," Rush said.

"The case of the stainless-steel frogs is, yes." The voice was

silent a while. *"How would you like to continue our arrangement?"*

"What arrangement?"

"I call your attention to crimes which I think need solving. You solve them. I pay you. Isn't that simple enough?"

"There's nothing," Rush declared, "simple about it. Who are you? What motive have you got? Why, for instance, were you interested in this frog business? You haven't appeared in it anywhere."

"Believe it or not, I was intrigued because unusual crimes are my hobby. The theft of stainless-steel frogs seemed unusual. I read of you and your gadgets in the newspapers. It occurred to me to hire you."

"But what do you get out of it?"

"Satisfaction," said the voice, *"than which there is nothing stronger. The satisfaction of knowing that a wrong has been righted."*

"This still sounds crazy!" Rush grumbled. "Who are you?"

"Merely a voice. The voice of Bufa, who feeds on slugs, worms, and insects—human variety."

"But—"

"You will continue to put a light in Bufa's mouth at six o'clock each afternoon," said the voice.

"Listen here—"

"Good night." The unknown chuckled. *"An item in your morning mail may interest you."*

The item was a plain envelope containing nothing but the other half of the ten-thousand-dollar bank note.

DEATH IN BOXES

BUFA, THE TOAD, HAS A NEW
ASSIGNMENT FOR THE GADGET
MAN—AND IT COMES IN TIN BOXES

CHAPTER I

MAN IN THE
BROWN DERBY

THE MOUTH WAS too large. Too large to be handsome, but a friendly mouth. The rest of the man's face was a sunburned brown; the eyes were brown, the hair was brown, and the cheeks seemed to lie rather flat over wiry muscles, so that the whole effect of the head was alert and rather pleasant—except that the head had no body.

An electric fan sounded like a small airplane in the room. The room was hardly longer or wider than it was high, and the west wall and the ceiling were entirely window and skylight. Slow rain, the color of clam juice, squirmed over the glass. A large table stood close to the window and was covered with tools and material, but the next-size table stood more under the skylight and held more materials than tools.

Rush said, "Let's have a mirror."

The grubby man handed over a mirror. Rush stood it on the large table alongside the head, propping it up with boxes of materials. Then Rush drew the room's one chair to the table, sat down, and stared fixedly at the mirror. He stared at the head. He stared at the mirror. The head.

"There's not a doubt," Rush said.

"I don't think so, either," the grubby man agreed.

"It's sure enough my head," Rush said.

"Yes. It's your head." The grubby man was pleased.

Wind drove rain against the windows with futile,

sobbing force, while thunder coughed and went muttering away to the horizons; and out behind the window the brick and steel spikes of Manhattan stood in a drizzling vastness.

The grubby man asked, "Have you got the body?"

Rush nodded. "At my office."

The grubby man picked up the head and admired it. "A good job," he said.

"What do I need to know about it?" Rush asked.

"Not much. First, you fasten it on with this bolt." The grubby man indicated various small rods with hooks on the ends. "Connect these up to the controls. One rod moves the lips. Another will make it smoke a pipe. And so on. Easy to figure out."

"Swell. Put it in a box, will you?"

The grubby man put the head in a box, padding it with tissue paper, muttering something about keeping it away from any radiators, or the wax might melt and the head would lose its shape. "I presume," he said, as he handed over the box, "that you are a ventriloquist and are going to use this for your dummy."

"Begins to look like I'm the dummy," Rush said sourly.

"Eh?"

"Just—well nothing. Nothing at all."

He paid the grubby man seventy-five dollars, picked up his head and walked down a flight of old stairs. It was very dark on the stairs, and he stopped twice and used a flashlight beam to examine fresh, crisp popcorn strewn on the stair treads. He had sprinkled the popcorn there when he came up, and none of it was crushed. Evidently, no one had followed him up to eavesdrop on the negotiations over the head.

He ran madly through the rain toward the corner where he could get a taxicab.

Apparently, his dash took the man in the brown derby by surprise. He popped out of a doorway ahead of Rush, raced for the corner. Rush saw him.

"The fourth time I've noticed you!" Rush muttered. He stretched his legs—and began to overhaul the other. "I'll see who you are this time!"

The man in the brown derby looked back. The derby was too large and sat down over his ears. And that, with the fact that his dull-brown raincoat was turned up at the collar, made it impossible to tell much of anything about his face. He saw Rush gaining, and ran faster. They held about even to the corner, Rush looking for a dry doorway in which to cache his head while he ran.

The man in the derby had an old car waiting. He popped into it and left.

After he had stood in the rain and said a few things, Rush hailed a cab.

AFTER HE left the taxicab, Rush bowed his head against the rain, splattered through a gate in a tall shipyard fence, galloped, feet knocking up water, past a shapeless building of wood. Ducking under another structure which had a tin roof and four poles for walls, he tamped tobacco in a pipe with a long, straight stem and tall, black bowl, rather collegiate. After holding a match, he puffed smoke, cleared his throat, grunted, smacked his lips, and did other things of a man smoking a pipe with gusto. Ordinarily, Rush never smoked.

His new boat—not yet paid for—was clean and white in the rain. The boat was about as long as four automobiles bumper to bumper, and had two masts, the forward one higher—a ketch rig. It was a tubby boat, wide, a fat and comfortable ketch, which looked as slow as a sow in a mud puddle. Four springlines held her to the dock.

Rush leaned over the dock edge to bring a pointing finger toward one of four metal life lines on stanchions which encircled the boat rail like a fence. The electric spark which sprang snarling blue at his finger was all of six inches long.

After Rush had jumped up and down, snapped his fingers, stamped both feet and made faces, he picked up his pipe. It had flown out of his teeth.

He roved his flashlight beam over the boat. When the flashlight glare rested on the cabin skylight, he blinked it once long, once short, once long, and a faint green light began glowing in the cabin.

Rush made sure of the light, then took hold of the life line and climbed aboard, and nothing electrical happened. He unlocked the cabin hatch, but before he went below, he brushed the strong flashlight beam over the surroundings.

The man in the brown derby stood about halfway down the dock.

The light had taken the man in the derby by surprise, and he was turning his face away hastily when Rush saw him. The man began to run. Rush swore, nearly fell overboard in his haste to get onto the dock, and pounded after the man.

They knocked up geysers of water, stumbled over things. Both used flashlights. But the man in the brown derby got to his car again and got away.

"Damn!" Rush said, among other things.

HE STOOD scowling, then went back to the ketch, climbed aboard and went down steps into a cabin too full of workshop stuff and gadgets. The green light came from an emerald-tinted bulb on the control panel of the transformer which stepped up a high-frequency current for the prowler-discouraging electrified life line.

Rain floundered around on deck, shotted against the skylight; harbor water guzzled against the hull, a wave higher than others now and then making a bump that disturbed the whole craft.

Rush took off raincoat and sou'wester hat, and became a man with average height, but with nothing else average—he had the wiry, over-sinewy aspect of a circus aërialist. His plain business suit, tie, shirt, and handkerchief indicated that he seemed to like neat browns that matched his eyes and hair. The watch on his right wrist had a brown band.

The body on the stateroom bunk was an exact duplicate of his own over-sinewed frame, or as exact a duplicate as a good maker of dummies for department-store windows could create. The suit the body wore was identical with the one Rush wore. Rush worked for several minutes with screwdriver and pliers and got the head fastened to the body.

Then he gave attention to the toad.

CHAPTER II
BUFA

THE TOAD SAT on the stateroom table, greenish-brown on the back, yellowish on the belly, with a few warts, eyes of a tomcat; it was a foot high and half again as long, and had a gaping, red mouth large enough to take Rush's right fist—or the electric light bulb which he now inserted in the toad's mouth. The wire attached to the electric bulb ran to the cabin fixture, which in turn was plugged in on a city power-system socket on the dock.

Rush turned the bulb on. It gave off heat, and the heat caused a thermostat in the roof of the toad's mouth to close an electrical contact which turned on a wired radio "transceiver" in the toad's body. The "transceiver" began receiving from and transmitting to another "transceiver" located somewhere in the city. Rush knew all about the entrails of the toad. Such things were his meat.

He was Clickell Rush, called by the newspapers, the "Gadget Man." His fertile brain, chock full of electrical and chemical knowledge, had turned out thousands of inventions. "Most of them gadgets," said the newspapers, "for catching crooks and solving mysteries." The police hadn't cared for his gadgets enough to buy them. But he had found a strange market for them—as long as they were coupled with his services. The strangest kind of a market.

Rush frowned, leaned close to the toad and put out his jaw. He looked exasperated.

He said, "I'm getting right good and tired of this screw-ball-mystery business. I didn't like it when I found this toad in my room a month ago. And I don't like the rodent any better now."

The microphone in the toad picked up his voice and the "transceiver" put it on the city power lines, where it was heard somewhere by somebody about whose identity Rush did not have the remotest idea.

"Bufa," the toad said, *"is not a rodent, but a member of the species* Bufonidæ, *which feeds on snails, slugs, and other low life."*

"Nuts!"

"Aren't you satisfied?"

"No!" Rush said wrathfully. "You've got a hobby of spotting an unusual crime where there apparently isn't any crime. That's all right. Hobbies are dizzy anyway. But then you send me this toad so you can talk to me without my knowing who you are. That's queer. Because I invented a lot of gadgets for catching crooks, you want to hire me to solve the crime you think you've discovered. That ain't queer—it's screwloose."

"You did well on our first case," the toad said.

"That's swell," Rush said. "Now I quit."

"You quit?"

"I walk out!"

"Why?"

"Because I want to."

"But—"

"I don't know who you are," Rush said, "and I wouldn't like you even if I did."

"What is wrong with your temper this evening?"

"That dummy maker soaked me seventy-five dollars for the head."

"That," said the toad, *"seems a fair price."*

"I didn't say it wasn't. What makes me so hot is putting out my own money for such a silly-willie thing."

The toad said patiently, *"I advised you to have the dummy made because it is going to become necessary from time to time for you to apparently remain in one place when you actually do not."*

"Oh, no it won't," Rush said. "I quit."

"But you were paid ten thousand dollars for the first job you did for me."

"What's that got to do with it?"

"You got paid."

"I'll get paid again," Rush said. "I'll get paid ten thousand again or I don't make another move."

The toad protested. *"Ten thousand is a lot of money."*

"I've got a lot of life to lose. One doesn't lose half a life. It's all or nothing."

"What do you mean?"

"Meaning that I remember the kind of a mess your last job was."

"Look under me," the toad said.

Rush looked under the toad and found a piece of paper. He scowled at it. It was approximately one half of a ten-thousand-dollar bill.

The toad began to chuckle.

Rush put his face close to the ugly face of the amphibian.

"How did that get here?" he yelled.

"In about an hour," the toad chuckled, *"you will have a visitor. Accept his proposition."*

"Will he wear a brown derby?" Rush asked involuntarily.

The answer was slow in coming. Almost a minute passed.

"Hardly likely," the toad said.

"Who is the bird in the derby who is haunting me?" Rush demanded. "Is he connected with this?"

"Future events will show."

"Ah, rats! What did you say to do?"

"Accept his proposition. Then follow him and use your own judgment."

"My what?"

"Judgment."

"Suppose I haven't got any?"

"I thought you were quitting," the toad said.

"Maybe I will yet," Rush grumbled.

"You seem to be in a pugnacious mood today," the toad complained.

Rush said: "The only thing about this I like is that ten-thousand-dollar bill, and it's a zany—because only half the bill is here. For two cents I'd—"

He stopped. He could tell by the sound of the toad that the carrier wave of the other "transceiver" had stopped; that the voice of Bufa, the toad, had signed off.

CLICKELL RUSH, frowning at the toad, was not as mad as he sounded, because it was hard to stay wrathful with one half a ten-thousand-dollar bill in hand. It was mad of course, fantastic. But then, the gadgets he had invented were fantastic. The two things were in keeping. As for the other half of the bill, it would arrive in some fashion once the job was completed—or that had happened on the first case.

True, this present job was still vague. He was going to have a visitor; he was to accept the visitor's proposition; he was to follow the visitor and use his own judgment. "But why did this Bufa nut have to pick me out to work his trick ideas on?" Rush complained.

While he was thinking about people, his visitor arrived, jumping on deck, tapping on the cabin top. Rush opened the companionway slide and the man came down.

The visitor looked like a man with a proposition. He

looked like the kind of man who would come right into your office and say heartily, "I have a proposition for you!"

And it would turn out to be insurance, or an automobile or something. He was distinctly the salesman type, with a light gray hat, a large, amiable red face, and plump body in a blue business suit, and polished black-button shoes to which shiny drops of rain stuck.

And sure enough, he said, "I have a proposition for you."

"My name," Rush said, "is Clickell Rush."

"Yes, yes, I know." The visitor nodded heartily. "I saw some articles about you in the newspapers, including your picture. Quite famous you are, aren't you? The Gadget Man, you're called, aren't you? You invent unusual devices and use them to—do detective work—er—"

"My point," Rush said, "is—have you a name?"

"Oh, to be sure. Geoffrey Noahmer."

HE PRODUCED and handed over a business card which said Geoffrey Noahmer represented the Majesty Food Products Corporation of London, Glasgow, Paris, and New York.

"Englishman, eh?"

"Oh, absolutely." Noahmer had a little round paunch. He shook it with his laugh. "Yes, indeed. The fact is that I had heard of you and when a little matter came up, I thought of you at once. 'He's just the man for this,' I said to myself."

"You don't say!"

"Oh, absolutely. You are just the man."

"You tell me what I'm the man for, and we'll see," Rush said dryly.

"Oh. Hah, hah. You have a way about you. Quite." Noahmer called it "quate." He adjusted his subdued red necktie. "To cut the red tape and take the animal by the horns, as it were, we—ah—we are having a little competition difficulty."

"Competition difficulty?"

"Quate. Ah—you see, we manufacture a breakfast food preparation. Breakfast food. Extraordinary article, really. Very new. We have a prospective customer here in New York, a chain store chap, and jolly difficult to sell he is, too. Said for us to ship samples, and he'd test it; and if he liked it, he'd place a whopping order."

"And so?"

"Why, we shipped him the samples. They are arriving tonight on the plane from Bermuda."

"Plane, eh?"

"We wished to beat our competition. The time element was important. So we shipped the samples across the Atlantic by air."

Rush asked: "Where do I come in?"

"You get the shipment of breakfast food and turn it over to me."

"Get it?"

"Exactly."

"But didn't I understand you to say it was *your* company making the shipment?"

"Quate." Noahmer frowned. "One of our competitors poodled this shipment secretly. We just learned that his spies in our plant put cascara sagrada in the breakfast food. A physic, don't you know. Decidedly unfair tactics. So you see, we have to stop the shipment. We do not want to tell the chain store chap the truth. Might get him down on us, and all that. Perhaps mean we should lose an order of several hundred thousand dollars. Ah—you can see it is no small matter?"

"You mean," Rush said, "that the shipment was tampered with, so you want it stopped?"

"Exactly."

"Who is it addressed to?"

"Calvin Flow, 178 Sixtieth Avenue."

"How much do I get out of this?"

"Well—ah—let's say fifty dollars."

"Why not say five hundred?"

They dickered for half an hour and compromised on four hundred, after which the man who looked and acted like a salesman got his gray felt hat and left.

It had stopped raining.

CHAPTER III

STOWAWAY

RUSH PUT OUT the cabin light, went to the dummy in the stateroom, set it up in place, got it connected, and turned on the cabin lights again—moving as fast as he could. Then he went into the little forecastle. When he pushed against the apparently solid hull, a section opened, and he could crawl out of the boat and step onto stringers under the wharf. There were enough stringers for him to get ashore, by climbing from one to another under the wharf.

The man who had said his name was Noahmer was leaning against a shipyard shed, waiting for something. Finally, a small man came out of the murk and said, *"Es excelente, señor."*

"Is he still on the boat?" Noahmer demanded.

"Si, señor."

"You are sure?"

"Si." The man switched to poor English. "He ees sit in cabin an' smoke hees pipe. I am watch heem close."

Noahmer chuckled. "He fell for my story, then."

"Wheech story you use, *señor?*"

"The one about the packages containing breakfast food that a competitor had doped with physic. I hired him to get the packages off the plane tonight. Had to pay him four hundred dollars. The robber!"

"He ees to destroy packages, *si?*"

Noahmer said, "Sure. He is to destroy them."

Click Rush, standing fifty feet away in the darkness, holding a metallic gadget in one hand, a headset clamped over his ears, thought: "The fellow is a liar two ways by the clock. He lied to the Spaniard; what he told me was to bring the packages to him, not destroy them."

Then Rush got interested in what the Spaniard was saying to Noahmer.

"*Señor,* sometheeng ees seem queer to me."

"Queer?" Noahmer said.

"*Si.* You tell thees Rush to bring packages to you. But you tell me you ees ask heem destroy theem."

"I did, eh?"

"*Si.* I am close to boat an' hear you tell heem thees theeng."

"Eavesdropping! My word!"

"*Señor,* eef those packages are not destroy, eet mean many thousands of my people will die." The Spaniard's voice changed. It got low and guttural and full of grinding rage.

"We theek for long time you 'ave sell out to *Señor* Flow."

Noahmer said: "That's too bad!"

"Not bad, señor. Good! Eet ees knowledge which will save many lives."

"Oh, quate," Noahmer said.

HIS GUN must have been a foreign pistol with the sear filed or its mechanism altered in some other way, so that it was full automatic in operation, and fired as long as the trigger was held back. For it emptied itself in one blatting bawl, a goblin of flame leaping at its snout, and making a glow that showed the Spaniard doing a little dance with his face in agony and his hands grabbing at each new bullet hole that got into his body.

Click Rush was caught flat-footed, all tangled in the

wires of the parabolic-microphone-amplifier-headset gadget, several hundred times as sensitive as his unaided ears, which he had been using to eavesdrop. He got the outfit off, dropped it into a case at his feet, and ran after Noahmer.

But Noahmer ran to a waiting car and the machine departed. It was a coupé, colored, as near as Rush could tell, a shade of green.

Rush ran back to his ketch, where there was a telephone connected with shore lines; but instead of using the telephone to call the police and describe Noahmer, he looked at the cabin companion slide. It was open. He had left it closed. He yanked the slide shut and clicked the padlock. Someone began beating against the underside of the slide, beating furiously, wanting out.

Rush cast off springlines and hauled up the foresail. An offshore wind carried the boat out into the harbor. Rush stood at the wheel and listened to pounding in the cabin, heard the wail of police sirens reaching the Spaniard's body, and saw police emergency truck floodlights make the spot where the body lay as white as day.

Rush waited patiently while the faint breeze pushed against the sail, and when finally out of earshot of shore, he started the twin sixteen-cylinder motors. The slow-looking old boat got up and began to hit the top of about every third wave. Rush steered north and east, and when the boat was through Hell Gate, he shut off the motors and unlocked the companion slide.

There was a steady pounding below. He went down into the cabin and stopped a pale, scared Spanish girl who was trying to chop a hole in the bottom of the boat with the fire ax. She was a very small girl with very big eyes, but strong for her size, Rush discovered, in taking the fire ax away from her.

"Drowning us wouldn't be sensible," he said.

The big-eyed little girl seemed struck with astonishment; she blinked both large eyes at him. Then she went into the stateroom, peered at the dummy, and picked up one of the dummy's arms; then let it fall and go clunk on the stateroom table. As if the sound snapped something, the girl threw up her hands, screamed, fell to the floor, screamed again and began to squirm and tremble.

Rush said, "Now, now, don't take it that way!" and patted her shoulder.

INSTANTLY, SHE reached up and got him by the hair. She pulled his hair, gouged at his eyes, kicked his shins, tried to bite him, all the time whimpering and crying out incoherently. Rush tried to hold her, but one of her arms, or one of her legs kept getting away from him and finally he fell with her onto the bunk.

Grabbing a heavy blanket, he rolled her over and over until he had her wrapped. He tied lines around the blanket and the girl. It made an effective strait-jacket. The girl began to cry.

Whooping of a boat whistle and blistering profanity brought Rush out on deck, in time to steer out of the path of a big New York-and-Boston excursion steamer which was veering madly in the channel.

When the big boat had passed, Rush consulted the cabin clock, frowned, then adjusted knobs until a radio-speaker made static and said: *"Flight Four, Bermuda to New York, now over Montauk. Estimate land in twenty minutes."* The droning motors of the big transatlantic plane were faintly audible with the words.

Rush looked in at the girl. She was still crying.

He went out on deck, started up the thirty-two cylinders of supercharged power, and within an hour headed in toward Port Washington Airport, running past a "crash" boat which was idling off shore and past strings of lighted buoys. Rounding up to the crash boat wharf, he put out two lines.

"Is Flight Four tonight's Bermuda boat?" he asked.

An attendant said, "Yeah. It's due in twenty minutes or less."

Rush began to erect a tripod on the dock. It was of steel, and heavy like a tripod of the type used for motion picture cameras. On this, he mounted a large, complicated-looking thing which might have been a magic lantern having a large eye over a foot across and a smaller one an inch and a half across.

"You can't take pictures at night, mister," Someone remarked.

"This is a test of the imbecility interrogative percentage around here," Rush explained.

The other pondered. "Doesn't imbecility mean crazy?"

"Uh-huh."

"And interrogative—"

"Questions," Rush said.

The other sniffed and stalked away.

Rush kept the gadget he had mounted on the tripod focused toward the sound of big plane motors, which came out of the East.

CHAPTER IV
COMPLICATIONS

THE TRANSATLANTIC PLANE came roaring down Long Island Sound, picked up the seadrome buoys, squared off with the wind, boomed in and settled on the water, with the crash boat charging alongside like a snarling bull pup to be on hand if anything happened.

Motors gusting, the seaplane came to the ramp; her searchlights stuck out ahead like fat, white whiskers. The ground staff snubbed her up to the float, ran the gangplank aboard, and passengers began getting off. There were about forty passengers. Two pilots and a steward were last ashore.

Another gangplank meantime had been run to the baggage compartment and attendants were unloading luggage and transatlantic air express. Rush went over there.

"Representative of the company," he said, lying slightly. "Want to know whether you have a shipment for a party named Calvin Flow, of 178 Sixtieth Avenue."

The pilot said: "It's aboard. I remember them loading it in Bermuda. Two tin boxes, soldered shut."

"I'll wait"—Rush settled himself—"until you come to them."

They finished unloading.

"That's funny," the pilot said.

"It won't be funny if that shipment isn't aboard," Rush said.

"Well, it's not."

"You mean there's no two tin boxes?"

"That's it."

"But you put them aboard in Bermuda."

That was sort of queer, they admitted.

While they were arguing with Rush, about how positive they were that the shipment was not aboard, and while the pilot was insisting just as emphatically that it had been aboard when they left Bermuda, someone shrieked. A weird kind of shriek. It tapered off in a noise something like a boot being pulled out of mud. Every one ran around looking for the sound.

Rush ran to his ketch, found the Spanish girl very still in the bunk, wrapped in the blanket.

"You make that noise?" he asked.

"No," she said in a low, sane voice.

Rush left her and raced back to help find who had made the cry.

It was the steward of the transatlantic plane. He sat in one of the large chairs in the observation veranda which ran around the second floor of the seadrome waiting room.

The steward's right hand held almost half of a bank note. With a tight inward feeling, Rush bent close to the bill—but it was not a ten-thousand-dollar note. It was only a five-dollar bill.

Turning quickly, Rush walked out. His stomach did not feel right, nor the rest of him, for that matter. It was the first time he had ever seen a man with his throat cut.

THE TRIPOD and the gadget which Rush had set up on the dock were both too unwieldy to take down quickly and get into the ketch cabin; but he did his best, got them aboard, then scrambled to cast off lines and start the motors.

While he was pulling away from the wharf, someone came running out onto the wharf and shouted, "Come back here! The police ordered everyone to stay at the airport for questioning!"

Rush gave the two sixteen-cylinder motors plenty of gas and went away from there.

He drove the boat hard for half a mile and all the time tapered off the throttles so it would seem he was going farther than he was. He continued into Manhasset Bay. At the end of the Bay, he cut the engines and let the boat drift. Rush went below. The Spanish girl stared at him. He untied her.

"Feel better?" he asked.

She nodded slightly.

Rush opened the gadget which had been on the tripod and removed the roll of film which it contained. He put this into a quick-developer tank. As the film came out, after passing through a whining drier, he fed it into a projector which threw each frame, enlarged, on the white cabin bulkhead.

He watched the changing pictures doubtfully. The part of the gadget that was not camera was an infrared projector sending out a ray of invisible light, but it was not effective any terrific distance, powerful as it was. Rush began to hold his breath, thinking the plane was not going to appear in the pictures at all.

Then the plane did show—the film was sensitive to infra-red light—and he clicked the projector with a finger, advancing the film a frame at a time, bringing the plane closer at an infinitely slower speed than it had actually arrived.

"This whole thing has got me mixed up," he told the Spanish girl.

She said nothing.

"Of course," Rush said, "I've got some of it figured. For instance: Something is being shipped from England, probably to Spain, via the United States. Whatever it is, it's in two tin boxes; and if it gets to Spain, a lot of people will die. They're having a war now in Spain, of course."

HE GLANCED at the Spanish girl. Rush said: "There also seems to be two outfits mixed up in this. One wants the shipment to go through. I think that group consists of Noahmer and a party named Calvin Flow."

The girl nodded slightly.

"You belonged to the other outfit," Rush told her. "Also the man who was killed. You are trying to stop the shipment. You came with Noahmer to hire me to stop the shipment." He frowned. "What I want to know is: who told you to hire me?"

The girl said, "The orders came from the chief of intelligence of the Spanish Loyalist Government."

"They did?"

"Yes."

"Then a fat chance I've got of finding out who the voice from the toad is." Rush glowered. "Whoever the voice of the toad is, he must have a lot of international contacts."

"Toad—international contacts?" The girl frowned. "Who are you talking about?"

"Skip it." Rush bent forward to watch the pictures. "After you and the man who was killed came with Noahmer to hire me, you learned Noahmer was double-crossing you; and then he killed your partner. You were scared and came aboard to get me. You found the dummy in the stateroom, and it gave you the willies and you went haywire."

"It wasn't the dummy," the girl said.

"No?"

"The man who was killed was my brother." She took hold of her face with her hands.

RUSH WAS silent. There was not much he could say, but he had a better opinion of the girl's sanity.

He watched the pictures. Something appeared below the plane. A dark dot, very small, and falling rapidly.

"That's it," he said loudly, enthusiastically. "I figured that they might know the shipment was to be stopped, and drop it overboard. And they would do that when the plane was close to the airport. That was the only time during the flight when they would be sure where the plane would be flying."

The dark dot blossomed out a parachute and sank more slowly. Rush said, "They paid the steward to get the stuff over the side."

The dot hit the water somewhere in Manhasset Bay.

"Then they killed the steward to shut him up," Rush said. He scowled. "This is all guesswork, of course."

"But how did they contact the steward?" the girl asked.

"There are radio-telephones, aren't there?"

He stopped the picture at that frame, dragged a harbor chart out of a case, and with a protractor, drew lines. He made a circle. "It landed about here." He made another circle. "And we're about here." He took hold of the girl's arm. "Out on deck, where I can watch you."

The night had become very still; the water was slick. Up against the stars, thunder was bumping, and a great mass of clouds slowly squirmed like a fabulous black dog growling and turning around and around for a place to lie down. Rush contemplated the water, the flasher buoys, other lights on shore; he compared them with the illuminated compass dial.

"East-northeast," he decided.

He turned the switch. The big motors began to rumble, and the boat put her nose up and flew across the bay.

"This is a deceptive boat," the girl said.

Rush agreed. "Got an underbody like a Gar Wood cup racer. It'll sail a little, too, with the centerboard down. What is in the tins?"

"We must be making forty."

"What about the tins?" Rush repeated.

"Tins?"

"The ones on the plane."

The girl was silent for so long that Rush began to think she was not going to speak.

"We agreed that you were not to know," she said.

"Why?"

"I—well—we'll say—international complications."

"That's great," Rush said. "Just great!"

CHAPTER V
THE DERBY AGAIN

A YELLOWISH LIGHT sprang up ahead. It turned blue almost instantly, and burned with intense brightness.

"Know what that is?" Rush asked.

The Spanish girl's "No," was hardly audible.

"Probably an ordinary chemical life-preserver flare that makes a light when water gets to it. You find them on ships—required by law." He was silent while he aimed the ketch at the blue light. "The steward must have stuck paper over the water inlet with mucilage, so that it took a little time to soak off."

The blue light came nearer. Rush saw that it was off the theoretical line he had drawn on the chart. Tide must have carried it more than he expected.

"How did your outfit come to take in this Noahmer?" he asked suddenly.

"The chief of intelligence of the Spanish Loyalist Government," the girl said.

"Him again?"

"Noahmer had cabled to Spain that he could stop the shipment, with the help of other agents," she explained.

"Which means you are a secret agent of the Spanish Loyalists?"

"My brother was."

Rush cut the engine speed to idling and jerked a boat

hook out of the cabin top rack. "You steer and do like I tell you." He went forward on deck. After about a minute, he said, "A spoke to the starboard—the right." A little later: "About another spoke." The blue light got so very bright that he shaded his eyes.

He missed with his first grab for the light, but got it the second time. The tangle of parachute shrouds made it easily snared. He hauled it aboard, detached the flare, and threw it overside, still burning, blistering his hands slightly in the operation. He scuffed a foot over the spot where the flare had blistered the deck. Then he explored the tin boxes with his hands.

They were about the size of the cookie tins in country grocery stores. Their combined weight was about seventy pounds.

It was very dark on the deck of the ketch, until he got back to the cockpit and a flashlight came on with blinding abruptness.

Geoffrey Noahmer's voice said: "Get in the cockpit. Sit down. Hold your hands up or do you want your insides blown out?"

The flashlight beam lowered enough to show the gun in the man's hand.

RUSH got in the cockpit and sat down and held his hands up.

"You got abroad at the seadrome," he said, "after killing the steward."

Noahmer said, "If you move, I'll kill you."

The Spanish girl sat very still on the other side of the cockpit.

Rush said to the girl, "Didn't you hear him?"

"No."

"Shut up!" Noahmer ordered.

Engine mutter in the distance, that at first sounded as

if it might be a motor car, grew louder and came closer, bringing with it rushing sound of boat bows cutting water. A craft came alongside, dark, long, a mahogany speedboat gleaming slightly in reflected glow from Noahmer's flashlight.

"Throw them a rope," Noahmer ordered.

Rush, standing in the flashlight glare, made a dry rope fast to the mast, then flung the end to a dark, squat man on the speedboat who took turns around a bow cleat on his craft. Rush walked back to the cockpit with his hands in the air. The speedboat swung broadside to the ketch, bumped the hull. The dark, squat man got bent over and ready to reach for the ketch rail. Another man, taller, but also dark, joined him and also got ready to reach.

The two men touched the rail at about the same time.

The tall man's scream was high and plaintive: the short man's was hoarse—a bullfrog croak. Sizzle of the electric spark was as brittle as glass ground together. Noahmer's gun, going off, made a great boom. Noahmer, distracted by the rumpus at the rail, had not seen Rush until Rush hit him.

Noahmer fell. Rush sprawled atop him. Rush got the gun, but it slipped out of his hands, entered the water. Rush got hold of Noahmer's hair. He pitched up and down, banging the man's head on the cockpit floor. Noahmer bawled and squalled and grew weak.

Rush went on bumping Noahmer's head with one hand. With the other hand, he reached into the cockpit seat box and began taking out bottles and throwing them at the speedboat. Some of the bottles broke; some went into the water without breaking. The bottles that broke let out gas and the two men on the speedboat—there were only two—began to cough and beat their chests and tear at their throats.

Rush, dragging Noahmer and pushing the Spanish girl, got down into the cabin. He yanked the slide shut, and closed two portholes that were open. Then he went back and knocked Noahmer's head against the Mainmast until the man slept. Sitting down, Rush breathed heavily and looked at Noahmer.

"Hardest head I ever saw," he puffed.

Later, he went out and tied ropes around the two help-less men on the speedboat.

THE POLICE were not very polite.

"You say that a toad told you about this in the first place?" a Captain of Detectives growled. "Do you think I believe that?"

"I don't care what you believe," Rush said. "That's what happened."

"But why did you get in it?"

"Curiosity," Rush said.

"Curiosity?"

"About whether the other half of a ten-thousand-dollar bill would turn up."

"Eh?"

"Never mind. You wouldn't believe that, either."

The officer said, "Get the hell out of here and let us and the District Attorney electrocute that Noahmer and the two guys he had helping him. Er—you know who this Noahmer is?"

"He's the man you're going to electrocute."

"Sure. But did you know he is also Calvin Flow, of 178 Sixtieth Avenue, who was pulling this thing. Mind you, he wasn't hired by the Spanish. He was hired by some country that wanted to see the Loyalists lose. We'll probably never know just who hired him. Anyway, it was the second time he had tried it. The other time he flopped, and you maybe read about it in the newspapers."

"That would be interesting," Rush said, "if it wasn't all over with."

"All right, you might as well beat it."

"What about the boxes?"

"They'll be destroyed. The officer scowled. "Don't think they won't."

Rush got up, put on his hat and grinned at the assembled policemen.

"What gets me," he said, "is this: We didn't catch anybody wearing a brown derby."

"We caught everybody," the captain said. "The Spanish girl says we did. She says there was only Noahmer, his two men that we got, and her brother and herself."

Rush shook his head.

"There was a man in a brown derby," he said. "He was beagling around after me at first."

"You were dreaming." The Captain of Detectives followed Rush to the door and shook hands. "You done all right. You're getting quite a reputation. The newspapers sure gave you a spread."

Rush thought so too. He bought all the newspapers he could find at the corner newsstand. The one with the biggest type said:

GADGET MAN SAVES MILLION LIVES
STOPS DEADLY GERMS

A more conservative paper said:

GERMS AMPLE TO
KILL MILLION PEOPLE
SEIZED BY CLICKELL RUSH
THE "GADGET MAN"

Rush read about himself in a taxicab, and was feeling

rather famous by the time he got back to the ketch. He turned the electrified rail off with the flashlight-photo-electric-cell-relay device, got aboard and entered the cabin. He looked at Bufa, the toad, first thing.

Then he sat down and talked to himself violently for a while. The toad was wearing a brown derby, and in the band of the derby was stuck the other half of the ten-thou-sand-dollar bill.

FUNNY FACES

THE GADGET MAN STICKS HIS
NOSE INTO THE CASE OF THE
MAN WITHOUT A NOSE, WHO IS
INTERESTED IN THOSE WITH NOSES!

CHAPTER I
ONE WITH A NOSE

THE MAN WHO was collecting noses had no nose himself. All the reports were quite generally agreed on this point. The collector did not have a nose and, as nearly as could be determined, he was a man who had once possessed a nose, but who'd had the misfortune of having his facial projection sliced off by some sharp instrument at some time in the past.

The fact that he had no nose of course made the man unusual.

But the fact that he seemed to be collecting noses off other men made him more unusual. His identity was a mystery. None of his victims knew him. The police were at a loss.

The fiend began his collecting early, in September, and the scene of his first operation was the park behind the public library in New York City; and the one who got his nose collected was a middle-aged man who kept a large telescope on a tripod on the sidewalk.

By paying him ten cents, you could look through the telescope at the Empire State Building, if you were an Al Smith Democrat; or at the moon, if you had the girl friend along. The man who had the telescope was grabbed, hauled into the park and relieved of his nose, at two o'clock in the morning.

The next nose came off a middle-aged taxi driver who got a call to come to the Bronx. This nose was probably the prize of the collection. It was unusually large.

The third nose came off Alec Drew, who was a telegraph operator employed by a press association on Madison Avenue.

These noses were collected during the month of September. In each instance, a razor-sharp implement was used. And in all the cases, the collector of noses was himself a

man who had no nose. He was also a short, broad fellow with reddish hair.

During October and November, there were no more collections.

Late in December, Clickell Rush came back to his trailer one afternoon and found an envelope fastened to the trailer door by thumb tacks. Inside the envelope was a plain white card and on the card these two typewritten words:

Get Bufa!

Clickell Rush tore envelope and card into small pieces, and threw the pieces on the ground. Then he jumped on the fragments until they were lost in the loose snow which covered the earth. Rush shook a fist in the general direction of all four horizons.

"Be blasted if I will!" he yelled.

A girl came out from behind a nearby trailer and stared

at Rush. She was a tall girl in galoshes, black caracul fur coat, and pert black hat. She had interesting eyes.

The girl's lips made, "Crazy as a loon!" without sounding the words. Then she walked away, glancing back twice as if getting away from something that might do the unexpected.

Rush got into his trailer and looked at a mirror to see if he looked as foolish as he felt. He was not in the habit of tearing up paper and stamping the pieces into the snow, then shouting defiance at empty winter air. It was an idiotic performance.

If the performance was idiotic, the reason for it was just as much so. The thing had started three months ago when Rush came to New York with several hundred devices which he had invented. They were unusual inventions, and Rush had hoped to sell some of them to the New York police department. But the police department hadn't taken his fantastic gadgets seriously.

The gadgets weren't as fantastic, though, as the big, greenish-brown toad Rush found in his room one day. Inside the toad was a "wired-radio" transmitter-receiver; and when Rush turned this on, the voice of an unknown man spoke from another transmitter-receiver somewhere in the city.

"I am Bufa," the voice from the toad had said. *"I feed on snails, slugs, et cetera—of the human variety."*

It was ridiculous, of course. Wild and silly business from start to finish, and Rush had been angry at himself for taking up the proposition the unknown voice offered.

The proposition was that Rush turn private detective and use his gadgets to solve a crime.

He had been angrier still when he had accepted a second job a few weeks later. He solved that crime, too, and he also made every effort to find out who was talking to him through the toad. But he didn't find out. The only satisfaction he got was a ten-thousand-dollar bill which he received on each occasion, half when starting on the case, the other half when he finished. Of course, ten thousand dollars was satisfaction not to be sniffed at.

On the other hand, ten thousand was a cheap price for his life. And on each of the other two cases, men had tried to kill him. Their efforts had been too expert for comfort.

Having thought it all over, Rush put the toad in storage with most of his gadgets. He was determined to accept no more weird jobs offered him by a voice from a toad.

He'd bought a trailer, fixed it up, and he was going to Florida for the rest of the winter.

Assuring himself that was exactly what he was going to do, he backed away from the mirror. The trailer did not have much room. His elbow hit his electric coffeemaker; it fell to the trailer floor, and the glass bowl broke. Rush looked at the fragments of the coffeemaker and realized that what he wanted most was a cup of coffee.

That was how he happened to go to the hamburger stand in the next block and meet the man with the funny face.

THE PARKING lot for trailers was located in a Long Island suburb of New York City, near the factory which had made Rush's trailer. Other trailers were parked in the lot, the owners of most of them preparing to head for Florida and escape the cold weather.

The hamburger stand was large, yellow, with glass on three sides, and it sat in the middle of a lot which was graveled for the drive-in business; but there was no drive-in business in this cold weather. Frost was like white paint on the windows.

Rush walked in with both hands over his ears to keep them warm, and kicked the door shut with one foot.

"Over your ears," the man with the funny face said, "is a good place to keep your hands!"

The gun he held was cheap and foreign. But if he pulled the trigger, it could kill whomever he was aiming at, if it didn't blow his own hand to pieces.

Rush looked at the man's face.

"Great goblins!" Rush said.

The man had an anteater nose. No other description fitted the proboscis. It was a finger-length longer than any normal nose, with skin of different texture and darker in color.

"Get over with the others!" the man said.

The others were the hamburger stand patrons aligned along the counter, holding hands level with shoulders. They were, with one exception, an average crowd for such a place.

The exception was a slender man who wore spats, a fur-collared overcoat and carried a cane. A white muffler was knotted English style at his throat. He wore a derby. The part of his forehead that the derby did not cover was wide, but his face wedged down sharply to a small mouth under a mustache that was a black eyebrow.

Rush got over with the others who were holding up their hands.

The man with the nose backed to the window, and with his left elbow scraped a patch of frost from the window. He threw a quick glance through the patch he had cleaned.

Rush watched the man with the strange nose. The fellow was strained, worried, on edge. He did not seem to know what he wanted to do next.

The derby wearer added: "He keeps asking for somebody named Click Rush."

"*What?*"

"He keeps asking—"

Rush called, "You with the gun!"

The man with the nose stared at Rush.

"I'm Clickell Rush," Rush said.

The well-dressed man popped dark eyes at Rush and began to back away.

"Prove that!" ordered the man with the long nose.

Rush was careful to make no jittery moves as be showed a driver's license.

"I was afraid they'd killed you already," the man said. "Let's get out of here."

They went outside.

A girl stood in the snow beside the door, a small automatic in her right hand. She was the girl who had said things about Rush's sanity at the trailer—the long girl with the dark caracul coat and the interesting eyes.

She pointed her small automatic at the man with the nose and said, "Drop that thing! We're going somewhere and you two are going to tell me what this is all about!"

The man with the nose whipped his gun muzzle at the girl and Rush grabbed the weapon. The gun made a violent crack in the cold air. Glass fell out of the lunch stand window. Voices yelled inside the place. Rush and the man with the nose went down. They threshed in the snow, and Rush got the foreign automatic.

It was then that the man without a nose appeared.

THE MAN with no nose leaned out of a car parked beside the stand. He must have been hiding in the machine, crouched on the floor boards. Judging from his shoulders, he was a squat man, and wide. The fact that his nose had been removed months ago—there was healed scar-tissue where the nose had been—gave his face a flat aspect and a hideous one.

He was an excellent shot. He fired before it seemed possible he could have aimed, and the bullet made the man with the long nose give one great jump and fall on his face.

The girl cried out, wheeled and raced through the snow, and fell down in her mad haste.

Rush went forward and down in the snow in a combined dive and slide that took him into the drift where the walk had been shoveled. He burrowed madly, trying to conceal himself. He could hear the noseless man's gun banging, and the bullets made rapping sounds in the snow and louder chops when they hit the frozen earth.

Then a car motor roared, tires made squealing noises in the snow, and there were no more shots.

Rush, very still in the snow, wondered if the man without a nose had gone away in the car. Or had it been a frightened onlooker?

Then the lunch stand door opened. Men came out and examined, judging from the sounds, the body of the man with the long nose. Then there were words by the man who wore the derby and carried the cane.

"He's dead! Shot right through the brain!"

"What was the name of the man he was asking for—the one who walked out with 'im?"

"Clickell Rush."

"Well, that's the fellow who killed him!" the well-dressed man said. "There is positively no doubt."

Rush got up out of the snow.

"That's enough of that kind of talk!" he said.

They stared at him as if he were a wolf that had jumped into a sheep pen. The way the well-dressed man ogled his right hand made Rush realize he still held the foreign automatic.

The crowd from inside the lunch stand thought he had killed the man with the long nose.

"I am going to call the police," the well-dressed man said. He took a step toward the door.

"Hold it!" Rush said angrily.

The well-dressed man lunged toward the door. Rush jumped, grabbed for him. He had bad luck, and the best he could get was a pocket of the man's fur-collared overcoat. He hung onto that. The pocket tore open, spilling the contents. The well-dressed man got inside the lunch room, slammed the door, got it locked.

Gloves, a handkerchief, and two small objects which glittered had fallen from the man's overcoat pocket. Rush picked up the glittering objects.

The things were about two by four inches and seemed to be two tiny booklets composed of a sheet of tin foil and two sheets of white cotton-flannel. On the tin foil, one word was stamped:

CONTOURESQUE

Rush put the two tin foil booklets in a pocket. There was no use trying to break down the door. He did a bit of mental calculation, and figured it would take ten minutes to get a police radio patrol car on the scene. Ten minutes was long enough to let the long girl in the black caracul coat get away.

Rush had an idea, he was going to need that girl badly, to prove he did not shoot the man with the long nose. He went looking for her.

CHAPTER II

ADVICE BY BUFA

THE YOUNG WOMAN'S long legs had traveled fast and made spaced footprints in the snow. These led around the lunch stand corner, thence across the parking lot, around a house which had boarded windows, across a vacant lot, then down a street lined with low-priced bungalows. The bungalow residents had not yet shoveled their sidewalks, and Rush followed the girl's tracks, without difficulty, to the point where she got into an automobile and drove away.

Rush stood there and stared at the prints of the car tires. The car had knob tires on the rear wheels and diamond treads on the front. The wheelbase, marks where it had been parked beside a drift indicated, was short. When the door had been opened, it had swung into the snowdrift. The door hinged from the rear edge.

Sirens on police cars made coyote noises in the distance, and the sounds grew louder. Rush turned up his brown overcoat collar. Suddenly he began running, and when he reached his trailer, he did not enter the trailer, but the car, a coupé, which was attached to it. He drove out of the lot, hunched over the wheel.

It was five o'clock, but the storage house where he had left his gadgets was open. He loaded stuff into the trailer until it was cluttered, and on top of the pile he placed a cardboard box heaped to the top with excelsior padding. Then he drove to another trailer park. Three other trailers were in the park, apparently none of them inhabited. Rush plugged the extension cord from his trailer into the park current supply.

Entering the trailer, he pulled excelsior padding out of the large cardboard box and lifted out Bufa, the toad that contained the wired radio transmitter-receiver. He had removed the batteries from the thing so they would not eat through and corrode the mechanism while he was in Florida. He put in fresh batteries. Then he inserted a lighted electric-light bulb in the gaping, scarlet mouth of the toad, turned the bulb on. The heat caused the thermostat inside the toad to close and actuate a switch which put the wired radio in operation.

"Hello," he said to the microphone in the toad.

A faint hissing sound indicated a "mike" had been cut in on another transmitter-receiver in some part of the city.

"You disobeyed orders," the toad said. *"I told you to get Bufa at once."*

The voice was so hollow that he was certain the other person was speaking through something, probably a hollow cardboard tube. Rush scowled. It was just as it had been before. He couldn't pick any definite characteristics in the voice.

"What gave you the idea," Rush inquired, "that any orders you gave would be obeyed?"

The voice from the toad began impatiently, *"You are working for me as a private detective—"*

"That's a mistake!" Rush interrupted. "I'm not working for you, and I'm not a private detective. I'm going to Florida, where it's warm!"

The toad made a disgusted noise. *"You'll go to an electric chair on the banks of the Hudson River which is considerably warmer than Florida, if you don't pay a little more attention to my orders."*

Rush said several things, all of them to the point, and ended with: "I'm through with you, whoever you are. I think you're crazy."

"Did you kill Charles Northrup?" the toad inquired.

RUSH FROWNED. "Who's Charles Northrup?"

"The man who was shot in front of that lunch stand about an hour ago."

"I didn't kill him!" Rush snapped.

"The police think so. They're looking for you for the killing."

Rush didn't doubt that. He rubbed his jaw savagely, and was about to say something wrathful when the loudspeaker in the toad started talking again.

"Have you heard anything from Saul Wagonetta?" it asked.

"No," Rush said. "Who is he?"

"What about Alec Drew?"

Rush inserted a finger in the collar of his shirt that was a brown matching the browns of his necktie, suit, socks, shoes and hat.

"Wait a minute!" he grunted. "That name seems familiar. I've heard it somewhere, maybe."

"You should," the toad said, *"cultivate a memory for the names you read in newspaper stories. Alec Drew is a telegraph operator who was seized on a golf course during September, and his nose sliced off. Saul Wagonetta was a taxi driver who was blackjacked in the Bronx in September, and his nose whacked off. And Charles Northrup operated a sightseer's telescope and he was hauled into the park behind the public library in September, and his nose was removed."*

"All right," Rush said sourly, "I remember it now."

"Each of these three men had his nose cut off by a man who himself had no nose."

"I told you I remembered it!" Rush snapped.

"*The nose collecting was a very strange matter, don't you think?*" the toad demanded.

Rush took a deep breath. "While we're at it, we might as well make it stranger. Charles Northrup, when he was killed, had a new nose, a very long one."

"*I knew that from the newspapers, which are already out with the story.*"

"I suppose you know, too, that the man who shot Charles Northrup was a short, wide man who answered the description of the man who collected Northrup's nose in September."

"*I'm not surprised,*" the toad said.

"You're not?" Rush growled.

"*The nose collecting, when it happened in September, looked like the beginning of an interesting crime,*" advised the voice of the unknown.

Rush said, "So it did!" sourly.

"*That is why,*" the toad said, "*I telephoned each of the three men who lost their noses and advised them to get in touch with you in case anything further of a suspicious nature happened to them.*"

Rush put his face close to the microphone and yelled, "Then that's why this Charles Northrup came looking for me this afternoon!"

"*Conceivably.*"

"What else do you know?" Rush shouted. "What is behind this crazy business of noses?"

"*That,*" the enigmatic voice said, "*is something for you to learn. I do not know. My hobby is watching the newspapers and picking out events which have more criminal significance than the police think. Through the medium of Bufa, who I admit is a trifle fantastic, but who I also insist is effective in keeping me unknown, and thus out of danger, I employ you to solve the crimes.*"

Rush was silent a moment, mentally kissing his trip to Florida goodbye.

"Is there a slender fellow mixed up in this? A man with a big forehead and an excuse for a mustache, who sports a derby, fur-collared overcoat and a cane?"

"I don't know. Who is he?"

"Is this all you know?" Rush demanded.

"All—except one simple fact, which you can learn by telephoning the homes of the three men who lost their noses in September," the voice replied.

Rush grimaced as he mentally accepted the fact that he would have to go ahead and see what he could work out of this mystery of the missing noses, whether he liked it or not. It was that, or let the police arrest him.

"All right," Rush said sourly. "Where's the half of a ten-thousand-dollar bill?"

The toad made a noise that was probably a snort.

"This time, there won't be any," it said.

"What?"

"This time, you have to do the job to clear yourself."

"But I've been getting ten thousand dollars apiece for these crazy jobs!" Rush complained loudly.

"This one," the toad said, *"is on the house."*

THE LOUDSPEAKER inside Bufa stopped hissing as the other wired radio outfit was switched off. Rush contemplated the device and rubbed his jaw. His wiry, trained leanness gave him a strained look that went well with his mental condition.

There were none of the five Metropolitan New York telephone directories in the trailer. He had not expected to need them in Florida. He went to the office-filling station-store on the corner of the trailer parking yard and was thumbing through directories which he found there, when someone came in with a late edition of a newspaper. The headlines were expected, but they had an effect on Rush's stomach regardless of that. They read:

CLICKELL RUSH HUNTED
AS NORTHRUP KILLER

Rush fingered in the "M" section of the directory for several moments before he discovered his mistake and went to the "N's." He called the Northrup residence. The grief in the voice that answered told him the death of Northrup was known.

"This is the detective department," he said. "Can you tell me anything that might help explain what has happened?"

"We don't know a thing," the voice assured him. "My husba… Mr. Northrup disappeared a week ago today."

"A week ago?" Rush grunted.

"Yes."

"And he is the Northrup who had the—er—misfortune last September?"

"That… that is right," the voice responded brokenly.

"Have you any idea why that thing was done?" Rush asked.

"No. None."

Rush hung up and chewed his lower lip thoughtfully. The man had vanished a week ago, had he?

He leafed through the directory again and found a Wagonetta, Saul, 108 Bundy Rd…. BUndy 76348. He called the number.

"Hello, poppa," answered an excited voice. "Is dot you, poppa?"

"I'd like to speak to Saul Wagonetta," Rush said.

"Oi," said the excited voice. "I am thinking it vas poppa is calling. Poppa is not come home for dis is de six days now tonight."

"Mr. Wagonetta has been away six days?" Rush repeated.

"Oi, and don't forget six nights, too. Say, mister, would you have seen poppa, maybe?"

"I'm sorry," Rush said, and hung up.

When he looked in the directory for Alec Drew's name, he made a discovery. Two Drews were listed with the same telephone number. Alec A. and Donna Drew.

"Donna Drew," Rush said, and thought of the long girl with the eyes. He frowned, muttered, "That's guessing, of course!"

He dialed the telephone number of the Drews.

"Hello?" a voice answered.

"Is this Thomas Jones's residence?" Rush asked.

"You have the wrong number," the voice said.

Rush hung up, certain he had talked to the long girl he needed to convince the police that he had not killed Charles Northrup.

He was grinning thinly as he ran out of the filling station. Two policemen stepped up and crowded against him from either side, and two more policemen got behind him and grabbed his elbows.

"This is the guy," one cop said.

CHAPTER III

BLACK FOG

PUSHING AND GRIPPING, the police jammed Rush
against the cold wall of the filling station. Their hands
whacked his pockets, under his arms, in the vicinity of his
belt. They pulled up his trousers legs and looked. A hand
slapped down on his brown hat hard enough to make sure
there was no gun hideout there.

"Clean," a cop said. He blew a whistle.

Two radio patrol cars came from side streets, sliding a
little on the snow.

"Great invention, the radio," Rush muttered.

"It's the age of inventions," an officer agreed.

"Including telephone line tapping." Rush sighed. "I
guess you had a tap on the wire, heard me call Northrup's
wife, and traced the call."

A policeman said, "Fast work, don't you think?"

"Mind giving me a cigarette?" Rush asked.

The officer laughed grimly.

"Well, then," Rush said, "mind if I smoke one of my
own?"

The officer grinned, got a pack of cigarettes from Rush's
coat pocket, withdrew one, broke it open and peered at the
tobacco. He looked at the other cops, his grin getting back
against his ears.

"Diphenylchlorarsine," he remarked.

"Huh?" Rush said.

"Don't be ignorant," the policeman advised. "There's tear gas in this cigarette."

"Watch 'im close," advised another policeman. "He's the bird the newspapers are calling the Gadget Man."

They gripped Rush's arms tightly and marched him toward the two patrol cars. They kept very close and were very careful.

Halfway to the cars, Rush carefully stepped on the heel of his right shoe with the toe of his left shoe. The heel came off his right shoe and was left behind.

Almost instantly, the shoe heel exploded. The report was gun-loud.

Rush croaked, "They've got me!" and went slack. But the policemen did not drop him. They turned clumsily, getting out guns.

The exploding shoe heel had ripened a great cloud of intense black vapor. This fattened as if it came out of the muzzle of an old-fashioned black-powder muzzle-loading cannon. It reached Rush and the police.

Rush jerked his arms. The cops were bewildered, and he got loose. He plunged into the black smoke. He kept his eyes shut, did not breathe. There was tear gas in the smoke, and he could not have seen anything inside it, anyway.

Going on through the smoke, he sloped around the corner of the filling station, running his best, and made for his trailer. He made the last dozen feet to the trailer in a slide, hit the trailer hitch, tripped it, and then went on to the car, dived inside and slammed the door. He started the engine, clashed gears and the coupé jumped away from the trailer, the front end of which plunked down in the snow.

He made time. All four wheels of the coupé were chained. He hadn't been taking chances on the icy pavement with the clumsy trailer.

He reached the Drew address in some odd seconds over eighteen minutes.

A SMALL sedan stood in the street. It had knob tires on the rear, diamond treads in front, and the doors were hinged at the rear edge, points which checked with what Rush knew of the car the girl had used for flight after the shooting of Northrup at the lunch stand.

The building was of a construction rather rare in New York—it was of wood. Practically all buildings in the metropolis are brick. The building was, judging from its lines, fifty years old at least. But it was a neat old lady. Paint was good, the flowers in the window boxes had been kept watered, and the brass doorknob had a neat polish.

Rush got out an envelope, scrap of paper and a pencil, fixed his mouth to say, "Special delivery for Mr. Drew," and knocked on the door. He knocked several times on the door without anything happening. He twisted the doorknob until he knew it was locked.

He walked around to the side of the house. A garage stood there, about fifteen feet from the house. The snow between house and garage was trampled with footprints. The garage was empty, the doors wide open. Lines of tire tracks grooved the snow from garage to street.

Rush studied the footprints from house to garage. It appeared that one injured person had been carried by several men and a woman. The injured one's hand had dragged in a place or two, and there were crimson spots.

The car in which they had all left was large, with tires almost devoid of tread, but with two mud hooks strapped around each rear wheel.

Rush went to the back door of the house. The door was open. He pulled it partially shut. From one pocket, he removed a square black block of a device which was equipped with four suction cup corners, a switch, two dials and a telephone jack. Rush clamped this to the door panel with the suction cups. He took a watch-case receiver out of another pocket and plugged it into the jack.

The door panel served as a sounding board, and the pickup amplifier magnified the sounds and put them into the watch-case receiver with great volume. Even the small rubbing of the clothing over Rush's chest, as he breathed, was audible as a great rasping in the device. He held his breath.

Four minutes of listening convinced him there was someone in the house.

"Special delivery!" he called. "A package."

No answer.

He went back to his car, selected a package from many other packages containing gadgets, and came back to the rear door.

"Special delivery package!" he called again.

When there was no response, he placed the package on the floor inside the door, stepped on it with his full weight. There was noise of glass breaking; the paper burst, and the package became a mass of foaming gray vapor.

Rush jerked the door shut and retreated, leaving the stuff inside the package to vaporize and spread through the house.

"We'll see what a fumigation accomplishes," he remarked.

WAITING, HE gave attention to the footprints in the snow between house and garage. He examined, particularly, marks other than footprints. There were a number of these, but three in particular interested him; they were perfectly round holes in the snow, about the diameter of a twenty-five-cent piece.

When he dug down carefully in the round holes, he found nothing at the bottom of them.

Having killed ten minutes or so outdoors, he went back and opened the rear door. He did not enter until he had tossed a chemically coated piece of absorbent paper into the place, and watched for a change in its color which would indicate the anaesthetic he had released in the house was still strong enough to produce unconsciousness. There was not enough change in hue of the paper to indicate danger.

Rush started searching the place.

The long girl was across a bed upstairs. Clothesline held her wrists and ankles; white adhesive tape sealed her lips and her eyes. The black caracul coat was across the foot of the bed, and her pert black hat was on the floor and wetly dirty where someone had stepped upon it.

In that room and in other rooms, there was evidence of a fight—upset chairs, puckered places in the rugs, a few gimcracks which had been knocked off tables and broken. In one place, there was a wet, red stain.

Rush, untying the girl and taking off the tape, saw the initials "D.D." embroidered on her frock over her left breast. There was an electric refrigerator in the kitchen, and Rush used ice cubes from it to assist a hypodermic stimulant to bring the girl out from under the effects of the gas. It seemed a long time before she opened her eyes and stared at him.

"You're Donna Drew?" Rush asked.

She nodded, still looking at him.

"Sorry about the gas," Rush said. "But I didn't know who was in the house, and I've kind of got an ambition to die of old age."

She felt of her mouth where the tape had been. The tape had left its stickum and her skin stuck to her fingers, so that there was a slight pulling sound when she took her hands away.

"Alec Drew your brother?" Rush asked.

"Yes," she said, her tongue thick from the anaesthetic.

"Someone came and got him?" Rush demanded.

She nodded.

"Who?" he inquired.

"One man—no nose," she said, part of her words sticking somewhere. "Others—masked—never saw them all."

Rush gave her a drink of water.

"What's it all about?" he asked.

She shook her head.

"But don't you know?" Rush demanded incredulously.

"In September—someone—my brother's nose." She coughed and kneaded her throat. "We didn't know—why that was done. Then someone telephoned us to get in touch with a man named Clickell Rush, if anything more happened that was suspicious." Her words came better since she had kneaded her throat. "Last night, someone tried to seize my brother again. So today I went looking for you."

"What did you want with me?" Rush demanded.

She looked at him. "I thought maybe you were the man who cut off my brother's nose last September. I was watching you at your trailer, and I saw you standing out in front of the trailer yelling that you would be blasted if you would do something."

"You thought I was crazy," Rush suggested.

"Well, you were yelling, and there wasn't any one around that you could be yelling at."

"You were at the lunch stand, though," Rush reminded.

"I suspected you of mutilating my brother. Don't you think I would watch you?"

"In that case," Rush said, "we're getting nowhere fast." He looked around. "Telephone here somewhere?"

"Downstairs," she said. "But what good—"

"I've got an idea," Rush said. "And what aggravates me is that the idea has been there some time, and I've been neglecting it." He pushed her back on the bed. "You get straightened out, and I'll call you."

He went downstairs.

USING THE telephone, he dialed the largest beauty shop in the city. He reached into a pocket, while he waited, and got out the tin foil cotton-flannel booklet which had fallen from the ripped overcoat pocket of the well-dressed man at the lunch stand. Rush gave attention to the name, *Contouresque,* stamped into the tin foil.

"Master Shops," a voice said in the receiver.

"This is Sergeant Slow of the detective bureau," Rush said. "I want some information."

"We'll be glad to oblige."

"Is there a permanent-waving machine called the *Contouresque?*"

"Oh, yes. A very good machine."

"And the permanent-waving pads, the little doodads, that are placed around the rod on which the hair is wound before the heating element is applied, would be stamped with the name of the machine, wouldn't they?"

"That is right."

"Now," Rush said, "isn't it a fact that good brands of waving machines, such as this *Contouresque,* are distributed one to a territory?"

"That is true."

"Where can I find a list of all the shops using *Contouresque* in New York City?" Rush demanded.

"We can furnish you such a list. As a matter of fact, we are quite familiar with the better shops and the individuals who operate them."

Rush got closer to the telephone. "That may make it simpler," he said. "Party I am looking for is a slender fellow with a large forehead, dark eyes, a trick mustache. Wears a derby, a fur-collared overcoat and carries a cane."

There was deliberation at the other end of the wire.

"Doctor Cuzard," the voice declared.

"Who?"

"Doctor Emanuel Cuzard."

"I thought operators of beauty shops were called *Monsieur*, instead of doctor."

"Doctor Cuzard is also a practicing surgeon, I believe."

"Now," Rush said, "the light is beginning to shine. What is Doctor Cuzard's address?"

"He lives over his beauty shop," the voice said.

An address followed.

"Thanks." Rush frowned. "If Doctor Cuzard should happen to be tipped off that we're inquiring about him, we'll know where it came from. People go to jail for things like that."

"Oh, gracious!" the voice said. "I wouldn't think of anything like that."

"Swell," Rush said.

CHAPTER IV

BEAUTY MAKER

THE SIGN SAID:

Doctor Cuzard, Inc.

The front of the building was modernistic blue and chrome. In the window left of the door was cosmetics; in the window to the right, an array of mannequins showing different styles of hairdressing.

The long girl took hold of Rush's arm very tightly.

"I work there!" she gasped.

"For Doctor Cuzard?" Rush demanded.

She nodded.

"Yes."

"Was he at your house today?"

"No."

"He carries a cane, and a cane had made marks in the snow at your place."

"That's strange," the girl said queerly.

Rush put out his jaw. "Did you know he was at that lunch stand when Charles Northrup was killed?"

She stared at him. "Was he?" She tied both her hands together in a tight knot. "He must have come there because I had told him I was going there to look for you!"

"You told him," Rush growled, "about me? For the love of little manicures, why?"

"He's always been very nice to me."

Rush looked over her curves, her eyes. "Being nice to you," he said, "doesn't prove a thing, except that a guy is qualified to wear pants."

He got out of the car, started to walk toward the corner with some idea of circling and getting at the beauty shop and the living quarters above through a rear door.

Then he saw the policeman across the street, looking at the license plates on Rush's coupé. The cop compared the pad numbers with a paper which he pulled from a pocket. Then he started across the street.

Rush changed his course, went to the beauty shop door. It was locked. He saw movement inside, pressed his face to the door, saw a man making for the rear of the place with some speed. The man had striped trousers, wore spats, and his general shape was that of Doctor Cuzard.

Rush brought the side of a foot against the door glass. The glass fell inward. Across the street, the cop yelled and began to run toward the beauty shop. Rush kicked twice more and cleared enough glass to pass him through the door. He went in.

Doctor Cuzard was going up stairs in the back.

Rush stopped, dipped in pockets, got out a metallic egg, threw it. The thing struck on the stairs, cracked open a charge of the black gas smoke.

Slackening his forward pace, Rush got out goggles of the type used by swimmers and snapped them over his eyes. He put a clip on his nose, inserted in his mouth a chemical filter effective against the gas.

It was very black when he got to the stairs. He felt his way up. There was noise at the top—a door crashing shut and a key rattling in the lock. Rush found the door. Steel, he realized when he hit it.

He used a syringe to squirt a liquid into the lock. Then

he shoved into the lock a wooden stick with a chemical on the end that was similar to a match with a thin shaft. He jumped backward, listened for the explosion, keeping his arms wound protectingly over his face. The blast roared. Pieces of door hit him, and he went forward headlong into the hail of fragments, and through the door.

He pursued Doctor Cuzard through a living room, a library, an office, and hit what was apparently a secret wall panel which the man was trying to close from the other side. The panel gave, and Rush and Cuzard piled onto a white floor.

THE WALLS of the room were whiter than the floor. There were no windows. Light came in a white glare from a celling flood, and directly under this stood a high table of chromium and black leather padding. There was a man on the table, straining up against the straps which held him. He was a long man, and he bore enough physical resemblance to Donna Drew that Rush knew he was Alec Drew.

There was a cot to the right, half behind a screen, and on this a man who was also straining against confining straps. This man was short, stocky, and the parts of his features which were not covered with bandages were Yiddish. Saul Wagonetta, was Rush's guess.

There were Instrument cases, anaesthetic tanks, and electrical devices around the operating table on which Alec Drew lay.

There were four men in the room. One of them had no nose. Two of the others had faces that It would be hard to like. The fourth man was Doctor Cuzard, and he was pawing through the instrument cabinet.

Rush rushed, hit the man without a nose headlong. The two of them went down. Rush rolled, managed to get into a corner, and held his captive in front of him. He was shielded for the moment.

He took a deep breath, yanked the filter out, yelled, "You'll hit your boss if you shoot!" and put the filter back again.

The other men had guns out. They hesitated. Rush got into his coat pocket, worked to get out another of the smoke-gas bombs. One of the men snapped a shot. The bullet hit Rush's arm, knocked his hand out of the pocket, and his fingers tripped the firing mechanism of the little bomb.

The bomb exploded, kicking his side like a mule. Smoke gushed, boiled. A little of it got into his lungs in spite of the filter, and he began to want to cough as he had never wanted to do anything before.

He threw the man without a nose aside, rolled to his feet. He was careful to keep inside the smoke. He felt about, when he touched a man, he twisted and struck furiously with the inside of his left elbow. The victim squawked as the hypo needle strapped under a sponge rubber pad on the arm drove out its stupefying chemical.

Rush felt around for another quarry. He could hear police sirens outside, loud noises of police below. Then he felt another form. He struck. This time, he missed. It was Impossible to see. Arms grabbed him. He knew, from the strength of the foe, that it must be the stocky man who had no nose.

Rush was hit in the midriff. He lost air out of his lungs, and the rush blew the filter out somewhere. He had to take the gas into his lungs. He began to cough and gag and feel terrible. With immense effort, he got away from the man who held him. He stumbled for where he thought the door should be.

It was then that someone hit him over the head.

AN AMBULANCE siren was making a great deal of noise when Rush was able to hear. He managed, by concentrating, to decide that he was in the ambulance. The voices must be in it, too.

"How did Nick Green lose his nose in the first place?" one of the voices was yelling.

Rush did not recognize that voice. But it sounded coppish.

The other voice, the frightened one, said, "He was trying to take over the policy game in Harlem. The men he was trying to take it away from caught him and cut his nose off. They said it would teach him to keep it out of other people's rackets."

That voice belonged to Doctor Cuzard. The man sounded very scared.

"You're a plastic surgeon, aren't you?" the officer demanded.

"I—yes," admitted Doctor Cuzard. "I—that is—"

"Sure, I know," the policeman growled. "We looked at your records. You've been doing face and fingertip operations for crooks. You operated on this Nick Green over a year ago, and neither the police nor the Feds were able to find him for some little things like murder and income tax evasions."

"I—er—"

"The answer," the cop said, "is yes. You'd better say it."

"Yuh—yes," quavered Doctor Cuzard.

"Why were the noses cut off those three men last September?"

Doctor Cuzard groaned "I had never done a complete nose graft. I explained to Nick Green that, before I tried to give him a new nose, it would be better to try out the operation on others."

"I hope they hang you!" the cop said.

"Nick Green couldn't find any men without noses, so he took a knife and fixed up some subjects for my first experiments," Doctor Cuzard moaned.

"They probably will hang you!" the officer declared.

"Charles Northrup got away from us," Doctor Cuzard said. "He went to this man Rush. He had heard us—heard Nick Green saying that we had better get rid of Rush, because a mysterious voice had told the men who lost their noses to call on Rush if anything else happened."

There was a brief silence. Then a fist gave Rush a violent gouge in the ribs.

"Ouch!" Rush said, and opened his eyes.

The policeman looked like a blue mountain.

"What about this mysterious voice that talked to the three nose-losers?" he demanded.

"Who got killed?" Rush asked.

"Nobody except Charles Northrup," the officer admitted. "What about that voice?"

"Did the girl explain that I didn't kill Northrup?" Rush continued.

"She said something to that effect. What about that voice?"

"Your guess," Rush said, "is as good as mine!"

The policeman pushed him back on the ambulance stretcher.

"We'll see if you've got any canary in you," he said.

"Canary?"

"They're used to singing behind bars," the big, blue mountain elaborated.

THEY KEPT Rush in jail two days. He had a good rest where it was warm, and the outside world experienced the coldest and snowiest blizzard in years. He did not tell anybody anything about the voice, because he did not know anything. It was the voice of Bufa, of course, and all he knew was that it was a voice over a wired radio hookup.

They turned him loose and gave him his trailer. He visited the long girl with the interesting eyes, learned to his disgust that she was engaged to another fellow, and lost what enthusiasm he had left for New York and its cold weather. As for the men without noses, Saul Wagonetta and Alec Drew, newspaper publicity had aroused the interest of reputable plastic surgeons, and they would probably get new noses as a result of the whole affair.

Rush headed for Florida in the trailer.

It was when he came back to the trailer from seeing Magnolia Gardens near Charleston, South Carolina, that he found a ten-thousand-dollar bill enclosed in a folded paper on the folding table inside the trailer. Writing on the paper said:

It was too good a job to be on the house!

Rush spent two days in an enthusiastic hunt for whoever had left the note and the money. He had about as much luck as the Ethiopians had against Mussolini.

THE SCARED SWAMP

BUFA HAS A NEW ASSIGNMENT
FOR THE GADGET MAN AND IT
DEALS WITH GRASSHOPPERS,
BUGS AND A BUGHOUSE!

CHAPTER I

THE GRASSHOPPER

CLICKELL RUSH WAS not ordinarily a swearing man.

But he managed to keep the Georgia air fairly blue for three or four minutes, did not repeat himself more than once or twice, and ended up feeling he had done the situation some justice.

Then he put the plug in the electric-light socket. There was a bulb on the end of the electric-light cord, and Rush put the bulb in the toad's mouth.

The toad with a mouthful of electric-light bulb looked ridiculous.

"Damn crazy business!" Rush said.

On its back where the warts were, the toad was green. Its paunch was mud-yellow. It had tomcat eyes. Rush had found from past experience that he could get it in a large traveling bag if he did not put in too much padding.

One of the pieces of paper the toad had been sitting on was green and had one torn edge. It was one half of a ten-thousand-dollar bill.

The other piece of paper was plain white with these two typewritten words:

TUNE IN

Rush waited for the electric-light bulb to heat the thermostat hidden in the toad's mouth, close a contact and thus turn on the wired radio "transceiver" hidden in the toad's body. Rush knew all about the toad's entrails. He had taken it apart often enough looking vainly for fingerprints of the man who'd given it to him.

Big raindrops hit the trailer windows like fat, juicy bugs hitting a windshield. Thunder overhead was giving a great

whoop an average of about two times to the minute, and lightning squirted glare somewhat oftener.

The trailer camp was as gaudy as the lightning. The advertising called it "Trailer Haven," and signs as far up as Virginia had started saying it was something to look forward to. They were right. Each trailer stood on a little numbered lot, on streets that were named. There were telephones, lights, water. There was a grocery, drug store, garage, movie theater, golf course, golf driving range, swimming pool, tennis court, and a *jai-alai* fronton.

It had been a swell set-up for a vacation. *Had been,* was right.

The toad began to purr as a microphone was cut in on

another "transceiver" plugged in somewhere on the city light system.

Rush leaned close to the microphone concealed in the toad. He said, "What kind of a fool business is it this time?"

The voice from the toad was strange. Rush had always been convinced the other disguised his voice by talking with a mouthful of pebbles or with a finger pulling his lips out of shape.

The toad said, *"I had hoped the change of scenery would improve your temper."*

Rush scowled at the toad. He said, "How'd you know I was here? How'd you trail me?"

The toad said, *"The man will be strange-looking. I think he is best described as looking like a grasshopper."*

Rush raised his voice. "I've resigned! I don't care what he looks like! I've quit this crazy stuff!"

"You will be interested in the plantation he has for sale," the toad said. *"But do not make the mistake of thinking the man is dumb because he looks queer."*

"The hell with it!" Rush said.

The toad chuckled. *"I am Bufa, of the species* Bufonidæ, *feeding on insects and slugs."*

The other "transceiver," going dead, made a click.

THERE WAS a small ax in clips over the trailer galley stove, and Rush stood and moved his gaze from ax to toad for some time. When he got rid of the impulse to use the ax on the toad, he put the toad in its traveling bag and packed excelsior around it.

He watched the clock blankly five minutes more, wondering who the voice of the toad could be. For months now, he had been finding those notes, and halves of ten-thousand-dollar bills, and the voice had been ordering him to solve strange crimes. Always, the assignments were cryptic. They told little; they were like the one just received.

A man who looked like a grasshopper was coming to sell him a plantation. There was a crime in that, somewhere, and Rush was to solve it, after which the other half of the bill would turn up in some unexpected place. Ten thousand dollars: A ridiculous price for a detective job! The crime would be fantastic, too. The others had been.

Rush got around to trying to figure out how the person he had not known, the voice of the toad, had found him.

He got out of the trailer. Rain beat him and he ran.

The man in the drug store said, "The late Savannah papers? Right there."

It was there on the front page, and it said:

THE GADGET MAN VISITS SAVANNAH

Clickell Rush, known as the "Gadget Man" because of his thousands of unusual inventions for catching crooks and solving crimes, arrived at Trailer Haven, Savannah's modernistic trailer park, yesterday.

Rush gained prominence recently in New York when he solved a number of remarkable crimes by use of his inventions.

The story carried over to an inside page, and gave a rehash of stuff the New York papers had printed weeks ago.

"Humph!" Rush said.

He went back to his trailer feeling rather famous.

THE MAN who had a plantation to sell did look like a grasshopper.

"I've got a plantation to sell," he said. "It's a bargain. A real buy. Something you can't afford to miss."

He said that while he was settling his fat body on a seat like a hen squatting down to set, and gathering in his long spindling legs. Then he took off his greenish hat, puffed out his cheeks and blew rain off the hat.

Rush did not say anything. Here was the first piece of the puzzle, and he hoped the rest wasn't as silly as this piece looked.

The plantation salesman had an undertaker's long face, and thin arms. Everything about him was thin but his body; that was huge. The gold watch chain angling across his vest was thin.

"I am Luther Gorman," he said.

"Mr. Gorman," Rush said, "I don't want to buy a plantation."

"But—"

"I don't want to buy anything," Rush said. "If I did want to buy anything, I doubt if it would be a plantation."

Gorman made a smile which showed yellow teeth that looked a little like they had been thrown at his gums at random.

"You act," he said, "as if I were selling life insurance."

"Do I?"

Gorman thought. His face went through a lot of antics while he thought. He puckered his forehead, and that made his long, yellowish front hair wriggle like a grasshopper's feelers.

"This plantation," he said, "is a buy you can't afford—"

"Who owns it?"

"I—er— What?"

"Who owns the plantation?"

The man exhibited his scattered yellow teeth. "I—Well—I am not at liberty to divulge."

"Who restricted your liberty?"

"I— What?"

"Never mind," Rush said.

He looks so dumb that it's pitiful, Rush thought. But he's the kind of an egg who can fool you.

The man gathered his long legs as if he wanted to jump, and the expression on his long face was that of not knowing which way to jump. He put on a patient look.

"This plantation," he began again, "is a rare bargain, one that—"

"No dice," Rush said.

"But—"

"A life insurance agent," Rush said, "would be a relief."

The man sighed. He took out horn-rimmed spectacles with

thick lenses and stuck them against his long face. His eyes looked like marbles in a fish bowl. He batted them at Rush.

"I'm sorry," he said. "I— Well, I'm sorry, and I guess I must be going."

He got up and took out of the pocket of his greenish coat a revolver.

"We'll go together, though," he said.

FOLIAGE WAS creeping nearer the road. Rush could tell that, because the limbs were beginning to bang the sides of the trailer. The stuff that sounded like snakes going over the trailer roof was probably Spanish moss hanging from limbs. Wind and rain pounced on the trailer in the open places and shook it and washed it.

Rush lay on his back and waited for the next big bump.

Wheels of the trailer under him kept parting loose gravel with a swishing sound, and flying stones hit the floor with sharp reports.

They hit a bump. The bump wasn't big enough.

The ropes around Rush's ankles hurt. They were tight. The man had wrapped the rope around the ax handle to get grip to yank them extra tight. Rush had reared up and looked at the ankles often enough to be sure the cords were buried in flesh. The ankles had stopped feeling as if they belonged to him. So had his wrists, for that matter.

The next bump was one such as he had been waiting for. He got high enough to root the ax with his head and it came out of the clips, turned over once, and the sharp blade cut the end of his right shoe smack off. It looked as if all toes had been cut off. The foot had no feeling.

Rush peered at the foot. He thought of what the colored boy with the razor told the other colored boy. "So yo' thinks yo' throat ain't cut? Son, just wait till yo' nods dat head."

He took his tongue with his teeth, then wriggled his foot. All five toes appeared, unharmed.

He worked with the ax until he had hands and feet free, then took out the gag. He studied the unscathed foot.

"Nice work, toes," he said.

The trailer stopped then. Stopped suddenly, and Rush went walking backward fast on his heels, trying to keep his balance, and his knees caught the forward bunk and he sat down with force, his head hitting the mirror. The mirror broke in large pieces which somersaulted onto his lap and onto the bunk.

He thought at first that the whack on the head produced the sound.

His next idea was that they had stopped at a plantation where a large group of colored folks were humming a spiritual. It sounded a little like that sort of thing sounded on the radio. No words; just humming. Subdued, not unmusical, rising and falling, with crescendos and diminuendos, but no pauses.

Rush frowned. He had rather taken it for granted that plantation singing was in the same bracket with cowboy songs on the ranches—something the movies always put in, but which rarely occurred in real life.

When the trailer door opened, the sound was more distinct, and all at once he knew he didn't have any idea what it was.

The "grasshopper" man yelled, "Have you got any tobacco?"

He held tight with one hand to the trailer door edge as if afraid it would get away. The fingers of his other hand kept going like a woman's knitting needles.

"Tobacco!" he howled. "Where's your tobacco?"

He sounded as if the one thing in the world he had to have was tobacco.

CHAPTER 11

THE SCARED ONES

HE MUST BE able to see that Rush was loose.

Thunder gave an excited whoop, and lightning turned all the raindrops pale red.

"Tobacco," Rush said, "isn't what you need, if you ask me."

The man wasn't listening. He had turned to half face the night. And, suddenly, he was shaking a fist at the darkness.

"Damned fools!" he shrieked. He whirled on Rush. "You hear that noise?"

Rush was hearing it. And wondering.

"I don't hear a thing," Rush said.

The man started, looked taken aback. Then he pushed his face at Rush.

"Ah—you think I'm crazy!" Then he popped his eyes at Rush. "Hell!" he said, astonished. "You're loose!"

Rush got the man by the neck before he could get his revolver. They got down on the trailer floor, went over and over and around and around while things broke or flew about. Rush got the gun.

The man got out of the door, and Rush crawled on hands and knees to the door, and pointed the gun at the jumping, plunging noises the man was making to escape.

Rush yelled as loud as he could, "Stop or I'll shoot your head off!"

The man kept going.

Lightning came and stood for moments in a white-hot and shaking streak, across the sky, and Rush aimed carefully and tried to shoot the man in the leg.

All the noise the gun made could have been equalled by a match stick breaking. After Rush opened it and saw that it was empty, he scrambled out of the trailer into the rain and threw the gun with all his force at the running man, and missed.

Rush ran after the man. They both made noises with their feet knocking up water. New lightning showed a stone path crowded by shrubbery, and showed the man taking grasshopper leaps ahead of his flying coat tails. And it revealed the house.

The house was a squatting old witch.

Gorman struck the front porch, slammed against the door and got it open. He went inside off balance, twisting to knock the door shut.

The lightning showed the narrow front of the house with the porch that was like an outthrust jaw, the two oval windows above with little scabby, shingled porches over them like eyebrows, and the rambling rest of the building beyond that made up the rest of the witch.

Rush went back to the trailer.

He listened to the weird humming sound that had terrified Gorman, while he put on a bulletproof vest and distributed gadgets through his clothing. After he was, as he reflected wryly, "loaded for bear," he stood in the door of the trailer with a parabolic microphone of extreme sensitivity and an amplifier of great power. This listening device was connected to a telephonic headset he wore. In the headset, the raindrops bursting on leaves were like bombshells, and the thunder was an earthquake.

The device was a pint-size edition of the contraption perfected by the army for spotting planes by sound.

Having listened to the humming for three or four minutes, Rush knew no more about it than he did before.

He said, "Blast the rain!"

Then he went to the house, walked in the front door and looked in surprise at the girl standing holding the telephone.

THE ROOM was austere and dignified, paneled in mahogany. The wide staircase that swept upward was austere. The furniture was more antique than colonial, and dignified. The fireplace was a white and regal thing with gold-plated, or gilt andirons and screen, and it did not look as if the neat, correct fire burning in it could possibly give out warmth.

The girl was like the room.

"I beg pardon!" she said.

"Eh?"

"This happens to be a private home." She sounded cool and amazed beyond belief that any one should have the temerity to walk in.

Rush looked around the dignified place.

"Private, maybe," he said.

The girl put down the telephone with dignity. "Get out!" she said.

Rush looked at the girl's neck, wondered if it would turn out to be marble if you should try chewing it; then, he walked over and held the telephone receiver to his ear.

Rush was an average-size man with a trifle too many muscles that appeared to be made of piano wire. He had too much mouth. His skin was tanned brown, his hair was brown, his eyes were brown, and he wore, whenever he could, browns. He looked brownly astonished and put down the telephone.

"Dead," he said. "Wires cut or something."

"Get out!" the girl said.

"Where did Gorman go?"

"Who?"

"Gorman. You know—grasshopper?"

"I don't understand."

"He tore in here a few minutes ago," Rush said.

The girl looked utterly dignified.

"You must be crazy!" she said.

RUSH LISTENED to the sound. It was rising and falling, swinging up and down a musical scale, but certainly without a tune or any order at all. It wasn't like darkies humming, it wasn't like dynamos in a powerhouse, and it wasn't like wind around an old house. Not exactly. It was fainter inside here.

Rush dipped in his pockets. He pulled out five cigars in a box and took them out of the box; took out of his pockets cigarettes, a can of smoking and a plug of chewing. He put all the tobacco on a table with glass balls on the ends of its legs.

"I wonder if you would be interested in tobacco," he said.

The girl's hands went out in front of her. She ran across the room, holding the hands out. She was close to a table with little lion heads on the ends of its legs, when Rush saw that her hands were ready to grab at two dueling pistols that were inlaid with silver and lay in a purple, plush-lined case.

Rush galloped over and gathered the girl's hands and the two guns together with his own hands. They did a kind of a dance while the girl kicked at his shins. After she bit him, he took one hand out of the fight to get a small hypodermic needle out of a sheath and prick the girl's wrists with it. The pricks did not hurt her, but enough local anaesthetic was injected so that, after about two minutes, the girl's hands became useless.

She got back, looked at her hands, and began screaming.

She screamed steadily for all of a long minute.

Then the old man with the beard, the rimless spectacles and the cane came in. He had the cane hooked over his left forearm. With both hands, he carried a dignified silver tray on which was a neat linen napkin, a bottle of milk, a bottle of pills and a glass.

He said, "Time for your milk, my dear."

CHAPTER III

SPHINXES AND LIARS

RUSH PUT A dueling pistol in each hip pocket.

"Milk, eh?" he said.

The old man peered at Rush. The milk and glass and pill bottle began to make clinking noises as his hands shook them around on the tray. He placed the tray on the table alongside the dueling pistol case. Then, as if he couldn't see very well, he came closer to peer at Rush.

"I—why—gracious!" he said. "You're a stranger!"

"Good evening," Rush said.

"I— Well—good evening." The old fellow straightened his beard with one hand, then held to his cane with both hands. "Testell is my name. Doctor Ephraim Testell. I— Well—I preside here."

"You what?"

"Preside. That is, I am the resident physician."

"Oh."

There was close to a minute's silence. Then the old man turned half around, still holding to his cane, and looked at the girl. He made the pity sound with the front of his mouth that is also used to call hogs.

"Poor girl," he said. "She needs her milk."

Rush said, "She needs something."

The old man turned his head toward Rush. "You arrived recently?"

120

"Quite recently."

"I—ah—see. Did you— Well, did you want something?"

Rush shook his head.

He said, "I didn't want any of it."

"Any of what?"

"I'm wondering."

"Wondering?"

"I think so."

"Ah—I see." The old man smiled. "What is your trouble?"

Rush said, "I don't know. It's kind of like being stood on your head, then whirled around and around."

"I see."

Rush, exasperated, said, "Damned if I do!"

The old man made his hog-calling noise. "The man who brought you should have come in with you."

"Oh, he did," Rush said. "I sort of herded him in ahead of me."

"You—ah—I see." The old man's smile grew benevolent. "A violent case. *Hm-m-m!*"

Rush yelled, "Violent case? What the blazes is this, anyway?"

The old man came very close and peered intently at Rush's eyes. He looked puzzled.

"Show me your tongue," he said.

Rush stuck out his tongue.

"Goodness, I'm sorry!" the old man exclaimed. "I've made a mistake. I thought you were a new patient whom some one had brought."

"Patient?" Rush said loudly.

"Why"—the old man chuckled— "I don't believe you know what kind of an institution this is."

Rush nodded. "I believe that's one of the several things I don't know."

"It is an institution for mental cases."

"Bughouse?"

"Well, yes. Bughouse."

THE DIGNIFIED girl dashed forward suddenly, and while Rush stared at her in astonishment, she gathered up the cigars, cigarettes, smoking tobacco and chewing plug, held them tightly in her arms and raced out of the front door into the rain. She was gone long enough to get well soaked. She had looked as tense as a fiddle-string all over when she went out. She seemed more relaxed when she came back.

She said, "I threw them in the cistern."

The old man said, "Maybe they won't sink."

"I put them in a syrup can. I put enough rocks in to sink the can, and put the lid on."

"That's good! Goodness, yes!"

Rush said, "Everybody sure looks relieved."

The old man came over and took Rush by the elbow. Rush got his elbow loose in a polite way and stepped back. The old man smiled.

"Oh, I know you're not one of our patients," he said.

"That's nice," Rush admitted.

The old man cocked his head to the left side. "You—ah—haven't told me what I can do for you."

"The tobacco," Rush said, "puzzles me."

"Oh, tobacco." The old gentleman changed the cock of his head to the right side. "Isn't it too pitiful for words!" He moved his cane slightly toward the girl. "She has a mania concerning tobacco. She goes into hysterics at sight of it."

"Then she hides it, eh?"

"Yes. She always hides it. Always. Quite unusual, don't you think?"

Rush said, "Then you give her milk?"

"Well—milk, with a quieting medicine in it." The old fellow changed his head to the other side like a bird and blinked his eyes rapidly.

Rush pointed at the pill bottle. "Those pills are the medicine?"

"Yes. Exactly."

"Does Gorman," Rush asked, "get the pills, too?"

"Gorman?"

"The grasshopper."

"Oh, I—heh, heh—see!" the old man cackled. "So you met Gorman? He has the same fixation as this young woman. As a matter of fact, all my patients here have a tobacco fixation of some kind. We treat only such cases. This is tobacco-raising country, you know. People who go crazy here are likely to do so over tobacco."

"Very interesting."

"Yes, doubtless."

Rush pointed at the pills. "And you treat them with the pills?"

"Yes. I told you that."

"I believe," Rush said, "that you are giving them *formicoidea* in the *pantaleones*."

"Well—ah—a similar compound, yes."

"Something similar to *formicoidea* in the *pantaleones*, eh?"

"Yes." The old man nodded. "Exactly."

"*Formicoidea*," Rush said, "is a big word for ants."

"But—"

"And *pantaleones*—"

"But—"

"Is pants," Rush said. He walked over, picked up the pill bottle and spilled the contents on the table. "Furthermore," he said, "these pills are common beans."

"I—"

"Beans!" Rush repeated.

HE WAITED for some kind of a reaction—an attempt at flight, a fight, an explanation or more lies. But they just stood there, the old man and the austere girl, with their heads cocked to one side; and it was more than a minute before he realized they were listening, and that they had been listening all the time they talked to him. Straining themselves until it hurt to listen.

To what? To that strange droning noise outside in the thunder and lightning and the night. He could see that now.

Their fascination with the sound mesmerized him into straining his own ears at listening. He had studied the noise scientifically through his listener-amplifier device, and learned nothing, and listening to it now, he could tell nothing more about it, except that the thing had a species of weird fascination aside from the mystery which was clouding up around it.

After he stood there bewildered for some time, he discovered that his eyes had grown interested in the five toes of his right foot which stuck out of the end of the shoe that the ax had cut off in the trailer. He put his weight on that foot and water shot out from between the toes. He felt very wet.

He took a handkerchief out of his rubber-lined inside coat pocket, which was sealed almost airtight with a zipper, and held the handkerchief to his nose.

When he was sure he was inhaling and exhaling entirely through the gas-mask type of chemical pad which the handkerchief contained, he took a glass-walled bulb the size of a bantam egg out of another pocket.

The old man straightened up suddenly and looked very glad.

"Going away!" he said.

Rush presumed he meant the sound. It did seem to be going away.

Rush took the chemical pad away from his mouth and nose, and said, "I'd like a full explanation."

The old man stared at him.

"Young man," he said, "the kindest thing you can do to all of us is go away from here as quickly as you can."

"But—"

"Ask no questions, and go!"

The old man sounded firm.

Rush looked at the girl, and she appeared just as firm.

Rush put the pad to his mouth and nose again, made sure his breathing was right, and pegged the glass egg at the floor. It broke, splashed, and the splash evaporated in faintly colored vapor. It took a short time for the girl and the old man to drop down unconscious from the gas. They did not quite make it to the door.

Rush followed the muddy footsteps of Gorman. The tracks were extremely plain and easy to follow. They led back to a big and ancient kitchen, ended where the "grasshopper" had wiped his feet on a mop.

CHAPTER IV

TRAIL

H IS SEARCH OF the strange old witch of a house told him a number of things that were interesting, but not important until he came across the newspaper clippings. The house must be two hundred years old, and it was presided over by a girl who was neat; had money and a yen for fine old, austere things.

The name of the girl who owned the place was Regina Wintersett, according to the papers in her office. Regina Wintersett was the dignified girl lying unconscious from gas downstairs, judging from the picture in her boudoir. She'd probably given the picture to a boy friend, then spatted with him and got it back. It was inscribed, "To Cedric, from Regina," in a fine feminine hand.

But the newspaper clippings were the most interesting. The first one read:

FIELD OF TOBACCO VANISHES

The mysterious disappearance of a small field of tobacco has spread consternation among the employees of New Dawn plantation. It is reported that the tobacco patch was there one night, and gone the next morning. Hardly a leaf of the tobacco remained.

Complete mystery surrounds the disappearance of the tobacco field. It is said, moreover, that superstitious employees of New Dawn plantation are leaving.

Miss Regina Wintersett, owner of New Dawn plantation, curtly refused comment to an employee of this newspaper.

The rest of the clips did not add anything to that. "Tobacco," Rush said. *"Hm-m-m!"*

He went outdoors with a flashlight and slopped around in the rain, finding cabins and tobacco barns. Both cabins and barns were empty. Both appeared to have been in use recently. It looked as if the plantation employees had left, and all tobacco had been whisked off the place.

Later, Rush stood in the house and frowned at the girl and the old man. There was not much chance of them coming out from under effects of the gas for another half hour. It would not harm them, except that they might have headaches.

He sat down on the floor and occupied his hands with smearing the soles of their shoes with a dark, gummy-looking mixture which he took from a tin container that might have been a salve box.

By the time he had their shoe soles well smeared, he thought of a way of smearing the salve on the floor around them in a manner that would not look suspicious. He spread the salve on the floor. Then he got an oil lamp, sprinkled the oil on the rug, and broke the bowl of the lamp in the mess; after which it appeared that the rug was only wet with kerosene, even where the salve was smeared.

The way he figured it, the mysterious voice of Bufa, the toad, must have read about the disappearing tobacco patch in the newspapers. But what had caused the "grasshopper," Gorman, to come after him? Wanting to sell a plantation was probably a stall. He'd wanted Rush. When the plantation stall fell through, he'd used the gun to bring Rush. But why?

Rush went back to the girl's office to look for the reason. His first inspection had given him the impression she was the kind of a girl who kept everything that came through the mail or over wires. He'd noticed advertising circulars with dates five years old. She also noted down her telephone conversations on a pad in shorthand.

RUSH HAD studied shorthand, but he knew this was no guarantee that he could read the girl's notes, the beauty of shorthand being that the more expert you become, the more word signs, pothooks and curlicues you make up that mean words and phrases to you and nothing at all to anybody else. He had seen shorthand of speed champions that meant just as much to him as ancient Chaldean hieroglyphics. He did not know whether the ancient Chaldeans had hieroglyphics. Fortunately, the girl was not an expert.

He finally translated the pad leaf that interested him. He read:

> *Clickell Rush—trailer—Trailer Haven camp. Have to get him here by trick or force—After he is here, he will get interested and help.*

Rush looked at the shorthand he had translated and felt proud. He had, from the first, had an intense desire to learn the identity of the voice that spoke to him through the fantastic toad. Each time the voice had assigned him to one of the strange mysteries that it managed, somehow, to unearth, he had attacked the problem with as much desire to catch the owner of the voice as to solve the case. Each morsel of progress toward that goal elated him.

After a while, he decided the translation of the shorthand was no help at all in identifying the voice. It just told him that the voice had telephoned the girl—if that were what the notes meant. He returned to his frown.

The wait for the girl and the old man to revive was getting tiresome. He'd expected a search to yield more.

It still was not beginning to make sense.

The thunder and lightning and rain had ceased, and the queer singsong sound had gone away entirely. Suddenly curious about whether he could pick it up or not, Rush got the listener-amplifier, switched it on, and turned the controls up to full volume.

He thought he heard the sound to the eastward. Either the sound, or his imagination was good.

He was more certain about the man walking in the house. The fellow was in the basement—his careful steps were making the small gritty noises that shoes make on concrete. At intervals, there was a scrape, as if the man were dragging something.

Rush went downstairs carefully.

There was a man with a flashlight in the basement. The basement was modern and contained the farm lighting plant and a laundry. The man was inching a big wicker laundry basket carefully across the floor toward the door.

Rush crouched down and aimed with a little metal tube which was, mechanically, an air pistol without the adorning trigger and grips to make it look like an ordinary pistol. After the pistol made its spitting noise, the basket-dragger howled.

Rush listened to the words and noises of the man. The fellow said, "What the hell?" two or three times, then found the dart, turned the flashlight on it, after which he said, "What—what" and dropped dart and flashlight. Glass clicked on the floor as the flashlight extinguished and broke. A moment later, there was a soft bump as the man came down on the floor.

Rush walked down the basement steps and turned his

own flashlight on the man. The man lay with his eyes almost closed. Rush nudged him with a toe.

"Gorman!" Rush said.

The "grasshopper" man stirred slightly.

"You can talk," Rush said. "That local anaesthetic only paralyzed your lower body."

GORMAN OPENED his eyes wider. Hate showed all his scattered, tobacco-colored teeth.

"What's going on in this place?" Rush asked.

"Devil with you!" Gorman said.

The two men, one wire-muscled and tanned and alert, all in browns; the other big-bodied and gangling grotesque, scowled at each other and clashed wills.

"Devil with me, eh?" Rush said finally.

He went over and opened the basket Gorman had been trying to take away silently.

He said, "Ugh!" and closed the basket.

After he had stood back and looked blankly at different things in the basement until his insides got back to feeling the way they normally did, he got a stick, lifted the basket lid again, and stuck the flashlight beam into the basket from various angles.

He said, "Man or woman?"

Gorman did not say anything.

Rush said, "This happened sometime to-day, didn't it?"

Gorman was silent.

Rush asked, "What did it?"

Gorman still said nothing, but it was terror now that made his yellow teeth show.

Rush flung upon him suddenly and with pantherish violence, tightened fingers on the man's throat and bumped his head on the floor. "What killed that person?" Rush gritted.

The more he thought about the body in the basket, the

more his rage fanned. Horror at the condition of the body boiled up in wrath until he had a fanatic desire to maul this man who would not talk—

When calmness returned, he took his hands and his knees off the man. The fellow lay still, shaking a little, his hands clawing around over his clothing.

Rush glowered at the man's helplessness.

He said, "Too bad I drugged you."

The man said, "You didn't!" and lashed out at Rush's wrist with his right hand.

Rush felt the sting of the hypodermic airgun dart over a wrist vein before he knew that the man's hand held it, and after that they wrestled around on the floor for what seemed a long time before Rush's muscles stopped responding when his will ordered. He lay back, helpless, and wondered how the man would kill him.

Gorman said, "You've got another guess coming if you think it wasn't some job faking the effects of that dart when I didn't know what was in the thing." He did not sound particularly elated. He turned up the points of his vest briefly to show a wide, thick leather belt. "It hit that," he explained.

CHAPTER V
FEAR IN THE SWAMP

RUSH SPENT AN hour dragging himself to the basement stairs, up the stairs and through the lower rooms in the house, then up more steps and through the upstairs rooms. By that time he knew the girl, the old man, Gorman and the mutilated body were no longer in the house. By that time, he could also walk.

He tried out his walking ability toward the trailer. The trailer was gone. He went back to the house and tinkered with his little pocket ultra-violet-light projector, not much larger than a cigar case. The thing was mostly spring generator, for it took a lot of current. The lens, nearly black in color, had been cracked out of its mounting during the fight. He tried vainly to wedge it back in place, but finally had to hold it against the mount with his fingers.

He began in the big front room where he had met the girl, and where he had put the gummy salve on the carpet. When he turned ultra-violet light on the stuff, it turned to a pool of pale-greenish fire. The material was fluorescing under the ultra-violet light, glowing as do many chemicals.

Rush and three other people had walked through the stuff and thereafter left footprints. Rush followed the tracks. They were more blotchy outdoors, but could be traced.

They went into the swamp eastward. He covered half

a mile, and remembered that the strange sound had gone away into the east.

He got wet again, went all of two miles farther, much of the time on a path that must have been hard to build in such a swamp as was around about, and came to a fence. The fence surprised him.

Height of it was all of fifteen feet; the posts were steel, with insulators on which two different types of wire was fastened, one wire that was heavy enough that it could only be cut with very stout nippers or a hack saw, the other wire of a mesh fine enough at the base to stop a mouse, and not much more coarse at the top. A sign on the fence said:

DANGER
ELECTRIFIED FENCE

The luminous tracks went through a gate which was padlocked on the other side.

Having learned that much by sparing use of his flashlight, Rush went to work on the lock. The lock was cleverly wired, evidently with a burglar alarm. Having studied it out, he wired around it with copper strands that he got by dissembling part of the amplifying listening device. The lock was not hard to pick. He stepped through.

He was trying to make the gate look as if it were locked without it actually being so, when the girl rushed out of the darkness and tried to hit him with a club. He knew it was the girl as soon as he dodged the club and got hold of her.

"Psst!" Rush said. "You've got the wrong guy."

The girl stopped fighting.

"Oh!" she said. "I—I'm glad you got here!"

She did not sound dignified. Just plain glad.

A MOMENT later, she was jerking at his arm and urging, "Come! Maybe you can help Doctor Testell!"

Rush followed her far enough to get away from the gate, then stopped.

He said, "Explain things!"

"Oh, Gorman said if we came here, everything would be all right. He said you were scared and had fled from the plantation—"

"Gorman said I'd left?" Rush interrupted.

"Yes. He said that you had gone, and that if we came here and brought—brought Lane's body, everything would be all right after the body was disposed of. Gorman said I—I wouldn't have to pay the five thousand dollars."

"You wouldn't have to pay the five thousand, eh?"

"Yes."

"What five thousand?"

"Why, that's the money the man—it may be Gorman, and I think it is—wanted for not destroying my tobacco with Doctor Testell's bugs."

Rush took a deep breath. He said, "Er—bugs?"

"Don't you know anything about this?" the girl demanded.

"I've done some guessing," Rush admitted. "The guessing kind of runs like this: Somebody has some bugs, and they said they'd turn them loose and ruin your tobacco unless you paid off." He scowled abruptly. "That's plenty crazy!"

"That's what I thought at first," the girl gasped. "But I can't talk! Doctor Testell is—"

Rush said, "We've got to talk. Is this it: The bugs were turned loose on one of your fields to show what they could do. It scared your farm hands into leaving. The newspapers got the story. The voice of that toad read it and called—"

"Toad? What on earth are you talking about?"

"Never mind. Just a voice. It called you and told you to get hold of me to help out. The voice told me you'd have to finagle me into coming. You sent Gorman."

"I didn't dream then that Gorman was in on the extortion—"

"What happened," Rush interrupted, "while Gorman was coming after me?"

"Lane! They killed him with the bugs! Put tobacco on him. The things—ugh "

She sounded so much like she was going to scream that Rush shook her.

He asked, "Who was Lane?"

"The plantation hand who stuck with us," the girl choked.

"That scared you and Doctor Testell into pulling that stuff about a bughouse to get me away from the place, eh?"

"Yes." The girl sounded frantic. "I tell you, they're going to kill Doctor Testell if we don't hurry!"

Rush let her drag him along.

"Why?" he asked.

"Doctor Testell developed the bugs."

"Developed them? Developed insects to destroy tobacco?"

The girl stumbled, almost fell, and Rush helped her up again. She dragged him on.

"He didn't develop them to destroy tobacco," she said. "He just found out that he had developed an insect that craved tobacco. He thought he had an insect that would feed on boll weevils and nothing else."

"Then Doctor Testell is an entomologist?"

"Yes. He's worked for years for something to destroy boll weevils. There's millions in it."

Rush said, "Won't they hear us talking?"

"They're in the basement."

Rush went flat in the mud, and got up feeling his temper. He said, "I know—in the basement killing Doctor Testell. Why?"

"Because he knows about the insects. They were stolen from him by—by whoever is trying to get the money. I don't know who. I haven't seen him."

A house stood in the blackness before them.

RUSH PEERED at the house, but listened to a sound that was coming from the rear somewhere. It came only at intervals, and was something like the noise swarming bees make when a stick is thrust into their midst. It was, he decided, fragments of such a noise as he had heard earlier in the night.

"That the bugs?" he asked.

The girl's "Yes" was low. Her "Hurry up!" was louder.

Rush was interested in the insects. "How do they control 'em?" he asked. "If you turn 'em loose, I'd think they'd be gone."

"They're like bees!"

"Bees?"

"They have," the girl explained, "a queen which produces all the eggs. They always come back to the queen, exactly like bees. As long as you can keep the queen, you can keep the swarm." She jerked at him. "Come on! They left me tied upstairs. They may find out I got away!"

Rush let her lead him to a door, where he took off his shoes. The girl did the same. Then she led him inside and they listened.

"Basement," Rush said.

"I think so, too." The girl went ahead to the stairs. "They don't squeak," she whispered, and went down into an awful odor.

The basement was divided into a large room and a small one, and the larger, into which they descended, was electrically lighted and fitted out with four long tables and half a dozen tall cases with glass doors. On the tables stood small cages of fine mesh wire, glass-walled boxes resembling aquariums without water, and other stuff which was probably whatever an entomologist used. The cases held more of the same.

The door into the other basement room was at the opposite end of the laboratory, and was open; and they could see through it and make out two figures, but could not distinguish details about the figures because of a lack of light.

One of the forms lay on the floor with his shoes off. There was a pillow over his face. The other figure was standing on the ends of the pillow with both feet, holding it over the prone man's face. The standing man's hands held a wagon rod, the end of which was red-hot.

Each time the hot wagon rod came against the prone man's bare feet, there was a sizzling and the awful odor got worse.

The standing man put the rod down, got off the pillow, and the phone man's agonized moaning was audible.

"How much did you tell this Rush?" snarled the man with the poker.

His voice was so strained with the excitement of what he was doing that it was hardly understandable.

The man on the floor said he had told Rush nothing. He said it several times in different agonized ways that only a man being tortured could think of.

"I want the truth!" The other man reached for the poker.

Rush lost his caution and started a headlong rush across the basement. The man doing the torturing looked up. Then he snatched a gun out of his clothing. Rush got behind one of the tall cases as the gun banged.

The gun banged again, and all the lights went out.

RUSH YELLED, "Get back, girl! This guy's a sharpshooter!" Then he lay very still. He heard the girl jump suddenly, and get behind something. Wondering why she had not fled the basement, he turned his head and saw that the basement entrance was limned in light from the upstairs room, so that any one going through it would make a target.

The man with the gun snarled, "I had a hunch you weren't the kind who would get scared and leave!"

He fired his gun. He must have hoped the flash would show a target. It didn't.

There was intense silence until an object fell off a table, and Rush knew the man was advancing, prowling, hunting.

Rush went through his clothing as quietly as he could, hunting a gadget for the situation. It should be on him somewhere. He had pocketed it at the same time as the tin of fluorescing salve and the ultra-violet projector. It was a bottle— He found it in a side coat pocket.

The bottle had a narrow neck, and he got down with it close to the floor, removed the cork and switched it from side to side so as to throw the contents as far as he could, and as close to the floor as possible. Then he waited.

Two hot, red spots on the floor were first sign of the chemical working. Suddenly, the red spots began to go up and clap back on the floor. And the man with the shoes started screaming.

Rush was waiting for that, knowing the surprise would not last long. He rushed, closed with the other, searching with his hands for the gun. When he found it, he fought for that alone. The man kicked him, and Rush's legs began hurting from burns where the shoe soles landed. After the other's hold broke, Rush got the gun.

He hit with the weapon and the other dropped. After that, he felt out the location of the other's head carefully and hit again to be sure.

He said, "Girl!"

"Yes," she said.

"You might hold my flashlight."

THE COUNTY sheriff was a practical man. He wore large, square-toed shoes and a black hat, and smoked dark cigars.

"Ordinarily," he said, "I wouldn't believe a word of a thing like this." He took his cigar out of his mouth, frowned at it and suddenly ground it into the mud with a heel. "Ugh!" he said.

Rush said, "We poured gasoline over the bugs and set it afire. They're gone."

The sheriff shook his head. "Like I say, ordinarily, I wouldn't believe there were any bugs."

"Miss Wintersett can testify that there were," Rush said. "And so will Gorman."

"That's why I believe it. That is—I'll take their word. I don't know about believing it." He got out another cigar. "Let's put it this way: The part of me that is the law will believe it. That's enough, ain't it?"

"Enough for me," Rush admitted.

"Miss Wintersett," the sheriff said, "was always a truthful girl."

"And Gorman, too, eh?"

"Well, he saved your life, didn't he?"

"Probably," Rush admitted. "If he had told Doctor Testell I was in the New Dawn plantation basement, paralyzed from the effects of my own anaesthetic, the good doctor might have done something unpleasant."

"In which case," the sheriff grinned, "the doctor wouldn't have a fractured skull."

"Did I fracture it?"

"Afraid so."

Rush grinned back at the sheriff. "Of course," he said, "Miss Wintersett and Gorman were really convinced some one had stolen Doctor Testell's bugs. I guess the doctor had given up his boll weevil ideas and decided to go in for extortion. He must have been a convincing old devil to put over his act as long as he did."

"I always liked him." The sheriff sighed. "Hell, and I'll have to hang 'im, too!"

The sheriff started fumbling in his pockets for matches. He brought out an envelope and peered at it.

"Hey!" he exclaimed. "I nearly forgot all about this!"

He handed the envelope to Rush.

"For me?" Rush said, astonished.

"Sure. Found it on my desk today. Addressed to you."

Rush opened the envelope and looked at the other half of a ten-thousand-dollar bill which it contained.

Later, the sheriff peered at him curiously. "What's the matter?"

"Nothing," Rush said, "that I have been able to do anything about."

WINDJAM

BUFA, THE TOAD, AGAIN CALLS ON
THE GADGET MAN—TO MAKE HIM A
FALL GUY FOR A MURDER FRAME!

CHAPTER I

THE MONKEY'S BUSINESS

THE VOICE OVER the telephone kept saying, "I'm Benjo Feldman! Blast it—you know me! Old Benjo Feldman!"

Clickell Rush used a left hand to hold the receiver against one ear. With the forefinger of the other hand, he gave the tip of his jaw a puzzled rubbing. He did not know any Benjo Feldman.

It was early in the night, sultry; grunting of distant thunder on Florida's warm air was making it hard to understand the voice over the telephone. Too, there was a little static on the line.

"What," Rush asked, "did you say?"

"I'm old Benjo Feldman—"

Rush said, "I don't know you."

"The devil you don't. You must have been pretty tight last night!"

Rush wondered if someone was holding a gun against the back of the man at the other end of the wire, or did it just sound that way?

He had not been tight the night before. He did not drink.

"Maybe I was kind of oiled," he said.

The other laughed. The laugh sounded as if it was hard to get out.

"Heh-heh," it laughed. "Don't tell me you don't remember the little bet on the sixth at Hialeah?"

"Was there a bet?"

"Heh-heh. So you don't remember it? Well, you laid ten bucks, and the oatburner came in at five to one. So you're fifty to the good."

Rush said, "Soft, eh?"

"Sure. You got time to drop around?"

"Drop around?"

"Sure. Drop around for the money. I've got it."

The telephone seemed to hold its breath and wait for an answer.

This is where I'm supposed to shoot, Rush thought, or give up the gun. What he wants me to do is say I'll be down for the money. But what I'd do if I had good sense is tell him I don't know him, never made any bet, and that it's as plain as the nose on his face that he's trying to stall me into coming down there because he's afraid somebody is listening.

Rush said, "Is there a toad mixed up in this?"

"What?"

"A toad."

"I don't understand what you mean."

"Never mind," Rush said. "Where do I collect?"

The voice was suddenly so glad it almost cackled.

"Come down to the big schooner *Fourth Wind* at Pier No. 4," it chortled, "and ask for old Benjo Feldman."

TO REACH the group of piers which is called the City Yacht Basin in Miami, it is necessary to cross Bayfront Park,

where the Miami moon can be depended upon to appear as represented, and where the air is balmy, the breeze rustles the palm fronds, and the air is fairly full of the big flying palm bugs that look almost exactly like large cockroaches.

When Rush was half way through the park, the stranger got up from a bench beside the walk. It was a gloomy and deserted spot, and the stranger, as far as Rush could tell, was dressed darkly. At any rate, his face was just murk under his hat.

He said, "Got a match, pal?"

Rush obliged.

The dark stranger took the book of matches and tore one off and struck it, and held it in his cupped palms with the palms opening away from him so that the match light got in Rush's eyes.

"Yeah," the man said. "You're Click Rush, the Gadget Man, ain't you?"

Rush said, "What's the gag?"

"No gag," the man said. "Old Benjo Feldman described you. We were to meet you."

Rush said, "I'm Rush."

The man said, "That's what I wanted to know!" and hit Rush over the belt as hard as he could.

Rush went down, got up, took hold of the man, and they both fell down and the man began to bark and bleat. He was hurt in so many ways and so rapidly that he tried several times before he got his words organized.

"Warner!" he howled. "The guy's tearin' me to pieces!"

Another man sailed out of the brush and joined the fight. It was too dark to tell anything about his face, either. All three of them wrestled around, punching and kicking and biting each other, and Rush managed to make it hard on them until something hurt his leg. It was a bee-sting kind of hurt.

Rush expected the hurt to get worse. Instead, it got smaller. Then there was a sting in the other leg. That one got smaller, too. All the different feelings in both his legs got smaller.

The legs quit working. They stuck the hypodermic needle into his arms and made more stings. They refilled the needle from a bottle and stuck him some more. After a while, he could not move or feel anything but his mind. They put a rag in his mouth and tied it there.

One man said, "How d'you like our gadget, huh?"

Rush buzzed through his nose.

The man said, "And I read in the paper that you were the wonder man of science. Hah! I'm laughing!"

The other man said, "Listen, B.T.U., we'd better get along with the egg sucking."

"Don't call me by name, you fool!"

"Huh?"

"Strip him."

They took everything that Rush wore except his underwear, and left him lying back in the park brush.

RUSH LAY on his back and looked up at the night sky between the tops of two palm trees that stuck up like a pair of clenched fists. A cloud like a dark animal crawled across the visible part of the sky and went on. After that, the stars seemed brighter.

Not until the girl turned on her flashlight did Rush know she was there. She might have been standing there for some time trying to make him out.

She was a medium-size girl, who had nice skin and a small nose, and who was slender enough that she probably did not have to worry about what she ate. She wore a raincoat of some dark-blue stuff that was as transparent as cellophane. The coat had a trick hood that came up over her head. Her hair was as red as a flame under the hood.

Rush, trying to tell her to help him, made noises some-what like a bumblebee in a box.

The girl turned around and ran. She went toward the City Yacht Basin.

Rush buzzed his loudest, but she did not come back. He remembered that, except for his underwear, he was as naked as a new-born mouse. That might have scared her. He was probably something to scare people.

He waited for the girl to come back with a policeman or somebody.

She did not return.

Nobody came for fifteen minutes or so; then the same two men who had attacked him returned with his clothes. They put them on Rush.

One said, "Hold him, Warner."

"Damn you!" the other said. "Who's calling names now?"

"Huh?"

"We'll get his fingerprints on the compass."

"Oh, sure."

One man grabbed Rush's right hand. The other held a five-inch boat compass which was shaped generally and sized about like one half of an ordinary cantaloupe. The compass was made of brass painted black, and had glass over the dial. They put plenty of Rush's fingerprints on the case and the dial.

"That oughta fix us up, eh?"

"Sure."

Both men ran off into the night, taking the compass with them.

CHAPTER 11

FOURTH WIND

In FIVE minutes Rush could roll, and he rolled to the path, then down it until he found three tourists who gaped at him and said, "Oh!" and "Ah!"

Rush said, "Heart! Taxi!" So they put him in a cab. To the cab driver, Rush said, "Pier Four, the schooner *Fourth Wind.*"

When they pulled up to Pier No. 4, Rush looked at the policeman on the pier.

"Changed my mind," he said to the cab driver. "Take me to my hotel." He gave the address.

At the hotel, the cab driver thoughtfully unloaded him at the side door. Two bell hops helped him to his room, and one bell hop said, "Brother, you sure got a load."

Rush peered at them blankly. "Did one of you unlock my door just then?"

"Nope. It was unlocked."

"That's the way it looked to me," Rush admitted.

He locked the door behind the bell hops. Then he stripped off his clothing, working fast. Naked, he was quite a different man than he was with his clothes on. When dressed, he looked like an ordinary man of wiry build and normal, or slightly under normal, stature. Only his carriage, or a second glance at his hands or his neck hinted at the kind of body he had. He was, undressed, like something made of piano wire with a sun-tanned skin painted on.

He started for the clothes closet, but veered over to stare at the piece of paper lying on one of his traveling bags which was nearly square. Two words typewritten on the paper said:

TUNE IN.

Rush picked up the paper in a way that showed he had a good idea of what would be under it.

"Damn!" he said.

He put the half of a ten-thousand-dollar bill that had been under the paper in his pocket without giving it a normal amount of inspection. From past experience, he had a pretty good idea it was genuine.

Then he got the toad out of its nest of cotton in the square traveling bag. The toad was about of a size to sit in a small washtub. It was ugly green on top, mud yellow underneath, and had warts. It was made of papier-mâché on a brass frame, and contained a small but very good wired radio "transceiver." Rush had dissected the thing several times hunting fingerprints.

The wired radio in the toad could communicate with another "transceiver" when both outfits were plugged in on the city lighting system. It did not matter in what part of the city either outfit was located, just so they were on the same system of power lines. The lines carried the signals. **RUSH PUT** the lighted bulb of the table light in the toad's mouth; this closed a thermostat in the toad, which switched the device on, and it began to hum as tubes warmed. Then "mike" noise indicated the other "transceiver" had cut in.

"*You're too late,*" the toad said.

"Too late?"

"*They've already got you.*"

Rush began, "Say, what in blazes is—"

"*You'd better step lively from now on,*" the toad interrupted.

"But—"

"*They got to you,*" the toad explained, "*before I did.*"

"Say, what—"

"*Good luck.*" The other transmitter went dead.

Rush glared at the toad with an overpowering impulse to smash the thing. It always affected him that way. The whole set-up was crazy.

Months ago, he had found the toad in the room with half a ten-thousand-dollar bill and instructions to tune it in, and the voice—he still hadn't the slightest idea who owned the voice—had assigned him to a strange crime to solve with his scientific gadgets.

The newspapers already had been calling him the "Gadget Man." He had solved that crime. Later, the same thing had happened several times, and he had solved those crimes, too. But it was fantastic. A zany.

But there was nothing that Rush had been able to do about it. Not, at least, as long as ten thousand dollars looked like a lot of money.

Anyhow, he seemed to be in this already.

He went on to the closet. He always wore browns. Looking through the closet, he wished he didn't. And finally, he decided on a sports ensemble of shades of brown as being most different, of what he had, from what he had been wearing.

He was buttoning up when knuckles gave the door a tapping. He did not answer the door. A moment later, they kicked the door down.

OF THE four men who came in, three wore the blue uniforms, white Sam Browne belts and white explorers' helmets in which Miami dresses her police.

The fourth man was wrinkled-looking in white linen.

He had heavy short legs, a thick body, a long neck and a long head. He had a physical imperfection of some kind in his bronchial system, so that a vocal cord seemed to be continually getting in the way when he breathed air out of his lungs, and caused him to make, at unexpected times, the noise that a pigeon makes.

The cops and the man looked around.

"Damned if we didn't get a break," one cop said.

Then he picked up the suit which Rush was wearing when he was waylaid.

"Mr. Cust," the other cop said, "is that the suit you saw?"

The man in wrinkled linen said, "I think I can safely say that it is."

"And the man?"

"I think I can safely say that is the same man."

Rush said, "This leads up to what?"

"Shut up!" a cop rapped out.

"But—"

One cop took out a blackjack. "Maybe you'd like to find yourself coughing up teeth," he grated.

Two policemen went over and looked at the toad.

"What's this?" one asked.

"A toad," Rush said.

The cop waggled the blackjack under Rush's nose. "Don't be funny!" he growled.

Rush complained, "And I was reading in a Chamber of Commerce pamphlet where it said Miami had the most courteous police in the world."

The cop said, "We fit our manners to the occasion."

They poked around the apartment and began going through the two trunks which contained Rush's gadgets and his chemicals. They started uncorking bottles.

"You keep that up," Rush said, "and you'll get our heads all blown off."

They left the corks in the other bottles.

"These trunks are sure as hell full of contraptions," said an officer. He came over to stare Rush up and down. "So you're the boy wonder?"

"The what?" Rush asked.

"The Gadget Man, aren't you?"

"In the newspapers, maybe," Rush admitted.

The cop said to one of his partners, "Hey, Joe! I read about this guy four or five times. He ain't a detective or nothin'—" He looked at Rush sharply. "Or are you a detective?"

"No detective," Rush said.

"See, Joe. He ain't a detective or nothin'. Yet he's turned up four or five times up north, in New York and them places claimin' to have solved some danged strange crimes. At the time, I figured him a phony. I says to myself, there's somethin' rotten in Denmark. This guy, I says, is puttin' somethin' over on them laws up north."

"But he built up quite a reputation up there," one of the policemen said.

"Hell, they give anybody a reputation up there."

A cop who had not spoken hitherto directed, "You bring that brown suit, Joe."

The policeman called Joe made a bundle of the brown suit. "I guess we take him to the schooner now, eh?"

"Sure. We gotta see if them's his fingerprints on the compass."

The man named Cust had stood back, saying nothing, making his cooing noises. He came over to Rush.

"Got anything to say for yourself?" he asked.

Rush looked at Cust. He looked at the cops. He looked at the brown suit.

Cust repeated, "Anything to say for yourself?"

Rush said, "Think not. Right now I feel like my Uncle

Pride's red hog must have felt when he got his head fast in the slop bucket."

THE SCHOONER was a hundred-and-fifty-foot example of what a very rich man can get if he is willing to put out money. Technically, she was a two-masted and gaff-rigged schooner with Diesel auxiliary, six-inch planking over four-inch frames and three-inch sealing. Artistically, she was something to take the breath.

They marched aboard her across a new gangplank of mahogany and chromium, which had probably cost a thousand dollars by itself. Then they went down a companionway into cool, conditioned air. They tramped along a corridor and stopped before a door.

Cust said, "I know you'll enjoy this!"

He opened the door. The police marched Rush inside. There was lots of good furniture in the cabin, but only the berth interested Rush. It was an ordinary berth.

The girl lay in a queer position on the berth. Her head was back, her neck was twisted, one arm was under her, and the other arm hung down in a way that it should not hang. Enough crimson had come from her nostrils to mess one side of her face.

Cust said, "You hit her plenty hard, didn't you?"

"Me?" Rush frowned.

"I suppose you don't remember it?" Cust said sarcastically.

A policeman growled, "You didn't expect him to remember it, did you?"

The cop called Joe said, "I think we've got a nice rubber hose that'll give him a swell memory."

Then the man with the jaw came in. For his height, the man with the jaw should have weighed a hundred and thirty or forty, but he probably weighed over two hundred. Fifty should catch his age. He had bright-blue eyes and a snub nose. To get such a rich-looking combination of blues, his tailor must have experimented a great deal. But his jaw was the most remarkable thing. It began close up under his nose and went out and down and back, like a sack of cement that had been wet and got hard.

He said, "I'm B.T.U. Bentrams!"

Then he waited as if he expected everybody to get down on their knees.

For a minute, Rush thought they would.

Rush said, "I met one B.T.U. tonight already."

B.T.U. Bentrams aimed the jaw at Rush. "Who's this?"

"I don't think the other B.T.U. was the McCoy," Rush said. "I think he was a gag to mix me up."

B.T.U. Bentrams began yelling. He roared, "Who's this?" and squalled, "By God, has the cat got your tongues?"

"We're not deaf," Rush said softly.

Cust cooed wildly in his efforts to make words.

"Mr. Bentrams," he said, "this is Clickell Rush, the murderer."

Rush asked, "Murderer?" He pointed at the girl on the berth. His voice got loud and angry. "What the hell are you trying to pull off? That girl isn't dead! I can see her breathing!"

The cops took hold of him. Their fingers seemed to be trying to bite in and get hold of his bones.

One cop gritted, "You'll look a damn long time before you see the man in the next room do any breathing!"

Cust said, "Sometimes they confess when they see the victim. Why not take him in?"

They shoved Rush into an adjoining cabin, where the wall paneling was black and a black carpet covered the floor. The berth had a black spread. Almost everything in the room was shades of black except the man on the floor, who was very white.

The man lay goose-winged. He wore the yacht-flunky whites of a man whose duty it had been to carry trays of drinks. And he had lived a long time before he died, judging from the wrinkles in his face.

B.T.U. Bentrams came in and stared fixedly at the dead man.

"Poor old Benjo Feldman!" he said.

CHAPTER III

THE POOR OLD FOOL!

RED LIQUID HAD come out of old Benjo Feldman's head through crushed places and spread over the floor, a surprising amount of red fluid to come from such a withered, little man.

B.T.U. Bentrams stopped himself from looking at the dead man by pinching his eyes shut.

"The poor old fool never hurt nobody!" he croaked.

Then Bentrams lumbered to the dark berth and sat on it, a stiff and tense figure with hands, fists, on his knees, and his mouth pulled out of shape so that it was an oval hole. Six or seven big tears got out from between his pinched lids. They fell on his jaw.

Rush looked at him and reflected that the worst sight in the world is a man crying.

"Is there a Warner around here?" Rush asked.

Cust demanded, "Are you gonna confess?"

"Yes, I'm going to confess," Rush said. "But I want Warner to hear it."

"You mean Doctor Warner?" Cust asked.

"How many Warners," Rush inquired, "are there around here?"

"Just Doctor Warner, the yacht's physician."

"I must mean him," Rush decided.

Doctor Warner was a tall bundle of bones with no

hair at all on top of his head and plenty of it on his face. His white beard was Vandyke, and his enormous white mustaches were waxed. He wore evening dress, with the white monkey jacket of the tropics.

He stared at Rush and said, "I never saw this man before!"

"I don't think I ever saw you, either," Rush replied.

Doctor Warner's mustaches bristled. "But Cust told me you said that—"

"I know," Rush interrupted. "But now I don't think the other Warner was the McCoy, either. I think he was put in to mix me up."

B.T.U. Bentrams roared, "You said that about me! What the blue blazes are you talkin' about?"

Cust came over and gave Rush a shove. "Come on, Gadget Man! You were going to confess."

Rush took a breath. "Sit down," he suggested, "and I'll give you all the gory details."

No one sat down.

"All right, hold your breaths if you want to," Rush grumbled.

He began by saying that a man named Benjo Feldman, who was scared, had tried to summon him by using a gag about a mythical race winner. He explained that two men who called each other "Warner," and "B.T.U.," had waylaid him in the park and borrowed his clothes for twenty minutes or so. He told about the fingerprints on the compass. He described the girl who had stood for a moment and looked at him lying drugged, adding that she was lying in the next room. He gave a minute description of the raincoat she had been wearing, but did not add that she was not wearing it now, nor explain that he was describing the raincoat because he hoped it would verify his statement that the girl had been there.

He told how he had gotten to a taxicab; said that he'd seen from the policemen on the dock that something was wrong, and had gone to his room to get rid of the incriminating suit, and also to move to some place where he would not be found.

"You see," he finished, "I had been framed."

THEY CLEARED their throats after the fashion of people who have listened intently to an argument and have a lot to say to prove it wrong.

"Why did you have to kill old Benjo Feldman?" B.T.U. Bentrams groaned. "He was such a harmless old duck."

Rush asked Cust, "Is he deaf?"

"Mr. Bentrams?" Cust said. "Hell, no!"

"I was explaining I didn't kill Benjo Feldman," Rush said. "I thought maybe he hadn't heard."

Bentrams snarled, "Are you crazy?"

"I don't know," Rush said seriously. "It's a question. I hate to think a thing as crazy as this could happen to a sane man."

Cust stopped cooing. "What was your motive?" he demanded.

"Motive for what?"

"Killing old Benjo Feldman," Cust snapped.

Rush said, "How was he killed, and how did you happen to pick me for the killer?"

Cust began yelling. He bawled, "I asked you what motive you had—"

Rush interrupted, "Let's don't begin braying at each other."

Cust screamed, "By damn, don't tell me what to do, you—you—"

B.T.U. Bentrams said, *"Mr. Cust!"*

Cust shut up as if his air had been cut off.

B.T.U. Bentrams said, "Mr. Rush, I was aft and heard

poor old Benjo Feldman yell. I ran toward the sound. I heard another yell. This yell was, 'Click Rush, don't! Don't do it, Rush!' And when I got to Benjo Feldman, he was like you see him now. Dead."

Doctor Warner gave his Vandyke a jerk. He said, "I was out on deck. A man ran out of a companionway and onto the wharf, and got away. He wore a brown suit and looked like you."

Rush asked, "Mr. Bentrams, are you sure it was Benjo Feldman's voice which yelled my name?"

Bentrams said, "I think so."

"You're either a liar," Rush told him, "or mistaken."

Bentrams put his jaw out angrily at Rush.

Rush said, "Doctor Warner, are you sure it was me you saw run away?"

"It looked like you!" Doctor Warner said with unexpected spirit. "And if you call me a liar, I shall be tempted to kick your teeth in."

Cust had been cooing by gusts. He bellowed, "If anybody kicks his teeth in, it'll be me!"

Rush peered at him. "Just what and who are you?"

"I'm a private detective," Cust roared.

"And what have you been detecting?"

Cust said, "I'm a bodyguard to Mr. Bentrams."

"And why does Mr. Bentrams need a bodyguard?"

Cust began, "Because—"

Bentrams said in a loud, interrupting voice, "Everybody in this damned country needs a bodyguard, what with kidnapers and gangsters!"

Rush said, "A patriot, eh?"

AT THIS point, another policeman came in carrying in one hand the black boat compass on which Rush's fingerprints had been implanted.

"We found this in the trash box at the shore end of the

dock," he said. "We gotta get a print man to bring out the latents."

Rush said, "Use cigarette ashes."

"Cigarette ashes?"

"They'll bring out latent prints on a black surface."

They did that. Cust produced a flashlight, unscrewed the lens and used it as a magnifier to compare the prints Rush inked on a paper with those the cigarette ashes brought out on the compass.

"Yours," he told Rush.

"Compass fits the wound in Benjo Feldman's head, too," Rush admitted.

Cust exclaimed, "Oh, I've got you, all right!"

"*You* have?" Rush said.

"I mean, *we've* got you," Cust corrected.

"Who is the girl in the next room?"

"Mr. Bentrams daughter—Nola Bentrams."

"Let's talk to her," Rush said.

"But—"

Rush said violently, "Somebody has made a fine attempt to shut up a man who wanted to tell me something by killing him. But it's going to be knocked higher than a kite when that girl tells you she saw me lying drugged in the park."

Doctor Warner went into the next cabin, came back and said, "Miss Bentrams feels able to talk."

They walked into the next room. The girl was sitting up with the aid of one arm. She looked at them as if it hurt her.

Cust asked, "Miss Bentrams, did you see the man who hit you?"

"No," she said briefly.

Rush asked, "Who is supposed to have hit her?"

"The man who killed Old Benjo Feldman," Cust said.

Rush stood in front of the girl confidently. "Miss

Bentrams, will you tell these gentlemen you saw me lying drugged and almost naked in the park a little before Feldman was killed."

The girl's eyes were blue. They traveled up and down Rush. She crowded her lips together, shook her head.

"You must be insane," she said. "I never saw you before."

WHILE THE shock of that kept Rush rigid, two of the policemen took hold of his arms. They held tightly.

Rush said, "But Miss Bentrams, you saw me—"

The girl got up, and holding her head with both hands and half running, half walking, left the cabin.

Rush said hotly, "This is a damned frame-up from A to Z, and I've had about enough—"

The policemen shook him. One said, "Enough! Hell—you haven't started yet!"

Rush began to jerk them around. They were too confident they could hold him, and in a moment all three men were on the floor. Another policeman and Cost dived into the mêlée.

B.T.U. Bentrams and Doctor Warner kept jumping around and looking willing to help. All the policemen and Cust managed to get Rush wadded up on the floor; but by that time Rush had managed to get his necktie out of his vest and the end of the necktie in his mouth.

When they dragged Rush up on his feet, he glared and chewed, his necktie as if that were the way he wanted to chew the men.

Cust snapped the necktie out of Rush's mouth. It hung down his vest, a damp ruin.

"We'll give you nice iron bars to chew on!" Cust said.

A cop growled, "We better throw his pants in the can, I guess."

He took out handcuffs and groped for Rush's wrists, but seemed to have difficulty in locating them. He began to feel around in search of the wrist. He bent over to peer.

"Hell!" he muttered. "Where's this smoke coming from?"

Cust made a cooing noise. "What smoke?" Suddenly, he put both hands out to one side as if the floor were going to tilt. "The boat is turning over!"

The boat was perfectly still.

There was no smoke.

After a moment, the policemen let go of Rush and fell down, and Cust fell also, more slowly; after which Warner and B.T.U. Bentrams fell.

Rush began to get purple in the face from holding his breath, so as not to inhale any of the odorless, quick-acting anaesthetic gas which he had released by crushing glass capsules of the stuff inside his necktie with his teeth.

He wiped the fingerprints off the compass with wild haste, ran out of the room, then resumed breathing.

On the dark side of the deck, which was not the wharf side, he found a rope, tied one end to a cleat and let the other end hang into the water.

He left the rope that way, walked down the remote gangplank to the wharf.

CHAPTER IV

THE HAND WASHERS

A STRANGE POLICEMAN was standing at the end of the dock to which the schooner *Fourth Wind* was tied.

Rush, walking past, said, "Good evening, officer!" in a loud, hearty voice.

"Good evening," the policeman said, after he had stared at Rush.

Rush rode a taxi to his hotel. There was no police guard in his room. He got a large, purple glass bottle from an equipment case.

He called the hotel telephone operator. "I want to talk to whoever you talk to to get an airplane ticket to South America." When he got the number, he reserved a passage on a plane leaving for South America in forty minutes.

He left the hotel, walked back to the City Yacht Basin and skulked out on Pier No. 4, which was next to the pier where the *Fourth Wind* lay. It was very dark. Rush was quiet about sliding down a dolphin to the water, and padding across to the rope which he had placed previously. He climbed the rope.

On the yacht deck he explored until he found a brass deck plate with the word "Water" stamped on it. He unscrewed this plate and poured the entire contents of his purple bottle into the schooner's fresh-water tank.

Then he hid in a lifeboat.

After about twenty minutes, there was some satisfactory excitement which came to a climax when it reached the cop standing at the shore end of the wharf.

The cop roared, "The whelp walked past me and spoke!"

All that end of town must have heard him.

Later, someone made a report in a loud, disgusted voice. "They traced him to his hotel. He made a reservation on a South American plane that just left, and they think he's on the plane."

Cust's voice said, "He's doing what I'd do if I was him."

There were ordinary ship noises for the next half hour or so. Then an argument broke out on deck between B.T.U. Bentrams and several other voices. Bentrams soon began hollering.

"Who the hell do you two-bit police flunkies think you're ordering around?" he roared.

"Mr. Bentrams," said one of the voices, "there has been murder, and we are asking you to be kind enough to remain in port until the investigation is completed."

Bentrams bawled, "And I'm telling you where to go jump! The government may take half what everybody makes in taxes, but I'm damned if it tells me when I can go fishing."

"But—"

Bentrams yelled, "Get off the boat!"

"Mr. Bentrams—"

"We're only going out in the Gulf Stream fishing," Bentrams shouted. "Be back in port tomorrow!"

There was more argument and the voices left, defeated.

Sailors finally cast off springlines; the Diesels started pulsing and the schooner backed out of the slip, then went into forward speed and moved past the channel markers and made the right turn into Government Cut.

Half an hour later, it passed the hooting sea buoy. The

schooner rose, fell, rocked a little with the Gulf Stream swell. Occasionally, spray came up from the bows and hit the deck like shot. After the sails were hoisted, the wind-jammer rode easier.

Rush climbed out of the lifeboat and went down a companionway into the main cabin. B.T.U. Bentrams, his daughter, Doctor Warner and Cust all opened their mouths except Warner, and the ends of his mustache stood up like startled ears.

Rush selected a chair and sat down.

"I've got an idea," he said.

CUST MADE his noise in his throat for a moment. Then he sprang out of his chair and yelled, "We gotta take him back and turn him over to the police!"

B.T.U. Bentrams said, "We haven't time to do that."

"Why not?" Rush asked curiously.

Bentrams, seeming not to hear the question, got up and came over to Rush and put his jaw out. He glared for moments.

"Damned if I make you out," he said. "Who put you wise to this? Somebody in Germany?"

Rush looked startled. "Germany?"

"It must have been somebody in Germany. It couldn't have leaked from this end." Bentrams jerked an arm at the others in the cabin. "Only these people here know about it."

Rush asked, "About what?"

Bentrams shoved his jaw out farther and said, "Ah-h-h!" disgustedly.

"Did old Benjo Feldman," Rush inquired, "know about it?"

"No; he didn't." Bentrams shook his head sadly. "And that gets me, too. Poor old Benjo didn't know a thing. So why was he killed?"

Rush said, "He was killed to keep him from telling me something. So he must have known."

"I didn't tell him." Bentrams looked at the others. "Did any of you?"

They all shook heads.

"See?" Bentrams growled. "He couldn't have known."

Rush said, "How's this for an idea: He heard somebody plotting against you, and called on me for help. So they had to kill him to shut him up."

"Why should he call on you?" Bentrams demanded.

"He must have got in touch with the voice from that damned toad," Rush said. "That's the only way I can explain it."

"Toad? What are you talking about?"

Rush said, "I don't know what means the toad uses to find out about crimes. Sometimes, he gets it out of newspapers. Other times—well, I don't know who he is or what connections he has. Maybe Benjo Feldman knew him."

"You mystify me," Bentrams complained.

"You mystify me, too." Rush looked at the girl. "Are *you* mystified by anything?"

The girl stared at him. "You talk like a crazy man!"

"I just wondered if the mystery was unanimous," Rush told her. "By the way, you're not a chronic prestidigitator, I hope."

"Prest— What?"

"Deceiver. Maybe I should have said liar."

"Oh." She thought for a while. "After we got back, I was going to tell them I saw you lying drugged in the park."

Rush said, "After you got back, you were going to tell, eh?"

The girl looked uncomfortable.

"We had to put out to sea," she said. "I didn't want the police to start asking questions and delay us."

Rush said, "I see," without enthusiasm.

"It was my idea," B.T.U. Bentrams said, putting out his

jaw. He scowled at Cust. "Cust," he said, "go up and tell Captain Ives to put on more speed. We don't want to be late!"

Cust got up.

Rush said, "By the way, when I came in here, I mentioned something about an idea. Let's go into that. Miss Bentrams, did you see the man who killed old Benjo Feldman, then knocked you out?"

"No," the girl said.

"How came you to find me there in the park?"

"I was just coming back from town," the girl said, "and heard you making noises. You startled me. I ran to the boat and rushed down to tell dad, and somebody hit me."

Rush sighed.

"Then my idea seems to be the only idea in sight," he said. He looked around. "Here it is: The suit taken off me in the park was worn by the murderer to throw blame on me. That suit was loaded with chemicals. You saw how the gas in the necktie worked? Just a sample. I think the chemicals in the suit the murderer wore might have left marks on his body." Rush rubbed his jaw. "That is, providing the killer hasn't already taken a bath."

B.T.U. Bentrams said, "That sounds kind of goofus!"

"How do you think this whole thing sounds to me?" Rush asked. "How about making some tests to find out if the suit marked the guy?"

B.T.U. Bentrams took out a gun and pointed it at Rush.

"What I'm going to do," he said, "is lock you up!"

BENTRAMS, HOLDING his jaw out, grating the snout of the gun against Rush's vest buttons, backed Rush out of the cabin and down a corridor. When the others started to follow, Bentrams roared, "I'll take care of this!" and drove them back with voice-violence. He backed Rush into a stateroom, came in himself and closed the door.

He tossed the gun onto the bunk and sat down beside it. He looked helpless.

"I don't know what the hell to do!" he groaned. "They're probably on the boat now. Damn it, you've got to help me! If you can find them, that might do it!"

Rush stared at him, "Who do you mean is on the boat?"

Bentrams said, "You probably doped it right. Poor old Benjo heard them scheming and called you, and they killed him to shut him up and framed you to get you out of the way. Now they're all set to rob me."

"I asked you who they are!"

The jaw drooped. "I don't know."

Rush, looking enraged, said in a loud, angry voice, "Isn't this something!"

"But you can find them with that chemical you told us about," Bentrams muttered.

Rush said, "There wasn't any chemical."

"What?"

Rush said, "That was a gag."

"But—"

"A gag. Maybe it'll work, and maybe not. We'll see." Rush went over and sat down beside Bentrams. "We've got a while to wait. Just when do we meet the boat?"

B.T.U. Bentrams looked blank. "Who told you we were meeting that steamer?"

Rush asked, "When did she leave port?"

"Sailed from Bremen, Germany, on the twenty-third—" Bentrams glared at Rush. "Damn you! You're pumping me!"

"Sure," Rush admitted. "All I know is that we wouldn't likely be meeting anything but a boat at sea." He grinned thinly. "Why do we meet this steamer from Germany?"

The jaw stuck out.

"Hell with you!" Bentrams got up. "I'm not afraid of them!"

He did not sound afraid.

Rush frowned at him. "Too bullheaded to get scared," he decided. Then he peered at the door. He registered dramatic, amazed suspicion. "*Sh-h-h!*" he admonished. "The door!"

He crept to the door, took hold of the knob, masked his hands and the doorknob with his body and took the key out; then he whipped the door open, jumped through, slammed the door, stabbed the key in the lock and got it turned. There was no one in the corridor, and he had not heard anything to lead him to believe there would be anyone.

B.T.U. Bentrams began to kick on the door, and Rush went into the main cabin. The Bentrams girl was standing close to a reading lamp, holding both hands under the light to peer at them.

She said, "What's wrong with my hands? They're turning green?"

RUSH WALKED to the girl, stepped around behind her, hooked both hands in the collar of her frock at the back and jerked, ripping dress and slip down the back almost to the waistline. He held the girl long enough to take a close look at her bare back.

When he turned her loose, she swung at him and he ducked; but she then kicked his right shin successfully.

He said, "*Ouch!*" and backed away, favoring the shin.

The girl said grittingly, "You *are* a maniac!"

"Just impulsive," Rush explained. "Wanted to see if your back was green, and I didn't feel like arguing up to it."

"My back green?"

"No, it isn't. Would be if you had taken a bath. I put some stuff in the water tanks that will turn green."

The girl said, "I don't understand."

"It's kind of a whacky idea," Rush said. "But if the killer

takes a bath to wash off the chemicals he thinks that brown suit left on him, maybe it won't be so whacky."

The girl backed to a chair, both hands behind her holding together the ripped part of her frock. She sank in the chair. "So that's it!" she said.

Rush asked, "Is this liable to get serious?"

"How do you mean?"

"Suppose part of the crew are in it, too?"

"They might be." The girl looked grim and uneasy. "Dad and I talked about that. It is very possible some of the crew are involved. If they are, I don't know what we shall do."

"We could just not meet the steamer from Germany."

She shook her head. "If the steamer went on, there is too much chance of it being searched when it reached port. The money might be found."

"Money?" Rush said.

The girl nodded. "Smuggled. About four million dollars, which dad received from his dye-making plant in Germany. The government of Germany would not let him take it out because dad is really a political exile, and still a German citizen. So he had the money converted into cash, smuggled onto a steamer, and we are meeting the steamer in a few minutes to get it."

"This," Rush muttered, "is a new one. A political exile smuggling his money out!"

"I think," the girl said, "that dad should have told you so in the first place."

Rush snorted. "Your dad is bullheaded. I can see why they exiled him."

Doctor Warner came in with his hands in the pockets of a long, dark coat. When he saw Rush, he took the hands out of his pockets with two guns. He pointed the guns at Rush.

"After I took a bath and saw my skin turning green," he

growled, "I saw through the gag you pulled."

He jammed his lips together and made his beard and mustache jump together.

CHAPTER V

JAM ON A WINDJAMMER

DOCTOR WARNER SEEMED to be waiting for something. He stood with his legs wide apart, hardly swaying with the lift and plunge of the schooner. If the guns in his hands moved, it was not enough to be perceptible.

A large, wide man wearing a suit of yellow oilskins came into the cabin.

"We got Cust," he said. "Tied him up and put him in the refrigerator."

Warner said, "Call a couple of sailors, captain."

"We've got to be careful," the captain warned. "There's fourteen men in the crew, and only three of them are ours."

"Get them down here. We've got to tie Miss Bentrams and this Rush."

The captain said, "You're sure the steamer will turn the money over to us?"

"They'll turn it over to Bentrams. We won't let Bentrams know anything until he gets the money. We can keep this quiet for another half hour."

"We'll meet the steamer before that," the captain agreed.

Three sailors came in and did an excellent job in tying knots in the ropes they wrapped around Rush and the girl. Then they carried both prisoners to the refrigerator, where Cust already lay on the floor, efficiently tied.

The refrigerator, as large as a cabin, was designed to keep

enough fruits and meats fresh for a long cruise. It was now empty, except for faint smells of its former contents. There was one electric light in the ceiling.

The three sailors, Doctor Warner and the captain of the schooner left, locking the door. They left the electric light turned on.

Cust bawled, "Doc Warner musta killed old Benjo Feldman!"

"It's tough we found that out," Rush grumbled.

"Tough?"

"Warner may hate to let us go on living."

They were silent, thinking about that. When the schooner's foghorn bellowed like a lost cow, they all started violently. The sound, heard inside the refrigerator, was very low. They began to yell for help.

But after five minutes of shouting, they knew it was not going to get results. The refrigerator walls were too thick.

By that time, the schooner had stopped sailing and was hove to. There were regular shocks as her bows bumped waves.

The girl said, "I believe they're meeting the steamer!"

Rush rolled to the refrigerator wall and began to scrape his heels down hard on the wall. After he had scraped for a while, one heel loosened enough to let two glass phials fall out. When Rush broke one of these, liquid poured out and made a sizzling noise and dense yellow smoke.

"That stuff is stronger than sulphuric," Rush warned. "Don't get in it, or breathe the vapor if you can help."

He used care dunking his rope bonds in the smoking acid. The stuff ate into the ropes, and when he could, he broke loose. He untied the others.

Cust got up, cooing angrily, and hurled himself at the door. It did not give; and there was no handle or latch on the inside.

"Solid as rock!" Cust complained.

Rush sat down and pulled his left trousers leg up off socks with elastic web tops. He tore the web top off the sock and carried it over to the door. He examined the door crack.

"Use hairpins?" he asked the girl.

"Bobbies," she admitted.

"Might do."

The girl gave him a bobbie pin, which he straightened and used to crowd strips torn from the sock-top into the crack along the side of the door.

He got the second bottle which had fallen from his heel, uncorked it, and it began to smoke. He dribbled the contents into the crack and over the strips of sock-top.

He got down on the floor in the far corner and hid his face as well as he could with legs and arms.

"You better do this, too," he advised. "That combination works about like guncotton. There may be splinters."

THERE WERE splinters. Also roar, jar, smoke. The electric light went out.

Rush got up, saying, "Be careful how you take hold of the door. That's the same kind of acid that ate up the rope."

Cust said, "Brother, I'm beginning to believe some of the stuff I read about you."

They shoved on what was left of the door, and it caved out on the third push. They followed it as it fell and confronted two sailors who were stumbling back out of the way of the door.

Rush decided neither of the sailors had been with Doctor Warner and the yacht captain.

Rush demanded, "Have they got the stuff from the steamer?"

One sailor said, "What happened here? They sent us to see what—"

The girl snapped, "Henry! Answer Mr. Rush's question!"

The sailor said, "They're hoisting some boxes on deck now. Small boat brought 'em over from the steamer."

"Where?" Rush demanded.

"Amidships. Port side."

Rush said, "Come on, Cust!"

He ran for the companion, and reaching it, realized the girl was following them. He stopped, told her, "This may be kind of rough for you."

"No rougher than it'll be if we don't take care of Warner and the rest," she said, and kept coming.

IT WAS dark on deck, except for flashlights stabbing bright cones at a pile of heavy wooden boxes stacked on the deck.

B.T.U. Bentrams was leaning over the rail, shouting something in German at someone who was answering back in German from a lifeboat in the water.

Doctor Warner held one of the flashlights. In the group around the boxes were the yacht captain and his gang of three sailors. They were not interested in the boxes, Bentrams or the lifeboat as much as they were in what report would be brought up from below. They discovered Rush almost at once, and pointed flashlight beams at him.

Rush got one arm up to hide his face before the light hit him. He extended the other arm, hand clenched as if it held something.

He changed his voice and shouted, "Captain! Look what I found below deck! Look!"

He got close enough to the captain with the ruse to hit the man on the jaw with all his force. The captain threw up his arms and went down, seeming to bend in every joint. Rush went on and tackled Warner.

Cust began fighting the three sailors, any one of whom was more than his match.

The girl screamed, "Dad! Warner killed Benjo!"

Bentrams turned around with his mouth open and slugged one of the sailors fighting Cust. The sailor rubber-legged backward to the rail and fell over it into the sea, and the men in the lifeboat began shouting excitedly in German.

Cust concentrated on one of the two remaining sailors, and by good luck, got his fingers in both the man's eyes, after which he could hit the sailor at will and with all his might. Bentrams jumped on the other sailor.

Rush got his fingers in Warner's beard and tried to hammer the man's head on the deck. Warner, by an athletic feat, managed to kick Rush in the temple with a heel. Rush had to jump up dizzily, still holding to the beard, and run backward dragging Warner by the beard, keeping the man so busy trying to keep his balance that he could not fight.

Not watching where he went, Rush crashed into the rail. Warner seized him, tried to get him over the rail. Rush held to the beard, yanked, struck, and both of them went into the sea.

Soon they were hauled into the lifeboat, and sailors sat on them and yelled at the schooner, wanting to know what they should do.

Later, B.T.U. Bentrams appeared at the schooner rail. He was dilapidated, but triumphant.

"Knock 'em cold with an oar!" he yelled.

Rush had barely started shouting before the oar came down on his head.

IT WAS an hour past dawn before the police came around to the point where they were willing to take the handcuffs off Rush. He rubbed his wrists, felt of the place where the oar had hit his head, and grinned.

B.T.U. Bentrams said, "How was I to know you fell overboard?"

Rush picked up the check which Bentrams had filled

out, and examined it. His grin got wider. He folded the check and put it in his billfold.

He said, "I'm not kicking."

A police detective came in and announced, "That yacht captain hasn't any guts to speak of. He's made a deal with the district attorney to testify against Doctor Warner."

"Damn the D.A.," a police lieutenant complained. "We could have hung Warner without any deals."

Rush buttoned his coat, shook hands all around and took a taxi to his hotel. He had a bath and shaved, then went down for the late editions of newspapers.

About half the front pages were covered with the story. The fact that B.T.U. Bentrams had paid Clickell Rush, the Gadget Man, a reward of twenty-five thousand dollars rated headlines.

Rush went back to his room feeling rather wealthy.

An envelope had been shoved under the door during his absence. He was not surprised. It was plain, but of very high quality. He had seen them before. One of them had arrived after each case assigned him by the unknown who spoke always through the medium of the toad.

The envelope would contain the other half of the ten-thousand-dollar bill.

He opened it. The half of the bill was there. Also, there was a piece of white paper with typewriting. The typing said:

> *Our agreement is that you get ten thousand dollars for each case. Therefore, you will give me the twenty-five thousand reward. Get the money in cash. Will advise later how you are to return it.*

Rush threw the paper on the floor, stamped on it, and said things in a very loud voice until the hotel manager whacked the door and told him that kind of talk wasn't allowed in the hotel.

Rush got a number on the telephone.

"When," he demanded, "is the next plane out of here?"

"You mean the Mexico City plane?" the voice asked. "That is the next departure."

Rush said, "Get me a seat on that one."

THE LITTLE MUD MEN

THE GADGET MAN THOUGHT HE WAS
TRAVELING INCOGNITO, BUT BUFA WAS
WAY AHEAD OF HIM TO ARRANGE A
MEETING WITH THE LITTLE MUD MEN

CHAPTER I

THE SAD CITY

C LICKELL RUSH CHANGED mustaches. He had put it off
and put it off, and now the passenger plane had started
down to make a landing, so he had to get the mustaches
changed. He ducked down between the seats and pulled
off the fake red mustache. He substituted a fake white
one; then examined the effect in a pocket mirror. It might
do.

The other passengers were too interested in the town
below to have noticed. Rush had made sure of that first.

From up here, this end of the town apparently consisted
of assorted red-and-green roofs, some narrow streets and
quantities of heat waves. There were a few trees, but these
looked discouraged.

As the plane got lower, Rush saw that the red-roofed
buildings practically without exception had white sides.
Farther over, there seemed to be tall buildings. It was too
hazy, really, to tell much.

It was not what Rush had expected of Mexico City. But
then, few things were what you expected of them.

He had changed the color of his hair earlier, and worn
his brown hat afterward. At the time, it had been simple
to go back into the washroom with a bottle of dye and a
comb and make his hair gray. He felt like an actor rigged
for an Uncle Tom's Cabin show, or maybe something out

of the funny papers. Still, the gag should work. The idea that it would work made him start grinning.

Nice to think about disappearing.

However, he did not believe Mexico City was going to be what he had pictured. He took another look through the window. The motors had slowed; the plane was very low, about to touch the landing field. It was a landing field which had two hangars that needed paint, and a runway pocked with holes big enough to bury dogs.

Whether Mexico City was what he expected or not, it would be all right if he managed to disappear in it. He had been trying to disappear for all of six months.

The plane bumped the ground, the wheels went in and out of deep holes, and the passengers held their hats. Someone said something angry about the air line supplying spurs with these crates.

When the ship stopped, Rush pulled his hat down, turned his coat collar up and got out. He was first out. The earth felt big and hard and warm under his feet. Good.

The pilot and copilot began unloading cases containing Rush's gadgets. The cases made quite a stack.

Without any of the other passengers getting out, the pilot and copilot climbed back in the plane. The ship turned around, roared its motors and went bouncing across the field until it took off; then made a diminishing noise going away through the sky.

Rush looked after it, astonished.

A voice behind him said, *"Buenos dias, señor."*

Rush turned around and inspected a large hat equipped with small bells. The man under the hat was short, wide, mustached, bright-eyed and the color of coffee with a little cream.

"Eh?" Rush said.

"Buenos dias."

"Come again."

"Hello, meester."

"Oh," Rush said, "hello!"

THE SHORT man shook his head and made a clucking noise of regret.

"Eet ees too late, *señor*," he said.

"Too late?"

"Sure."

Rush frowned. "Too late for what?"

"Thees funeral of Señor Juan Madarro. They holed heem yesterday."

"They buried who?"

"Madarro. Hees great man. *Mucho hombre*."

Rush decided he had never heard of anybody named Señor Madarro.

"Look," he said. "I didn't come to a funeral."

The short man shrugged.

"Eet was just guess, anyhow," he said.

Rush inspected the fellow curiously. "You got a name?"

"Sure. Presto."

"Eh?"

"Sure. Everybody call us 'That Damn Presto.'"

"Just what," Rush asked, "is your racket?"

"I got toxi-scrabs eef you want heem."

"Toxi-scrabs?"

"Sure. You want heem?"

"The use of imagination suggests that you mean taxicab. In which case, we might make a deal. How much to take me to one of Mexico City's better hotels?"

"Mexico City?"

"Yep."

"You ees mean *Mexico City?*"

"Yep." Rush pointed at the town beyond the airport. "There it is. Remember? You live there."

"Presto" got out brown papers and a muslin sack of

tobacco, and made himself a cigarette.

"*Señor,*" he said, "somebody ees crazy like bughouse."

"Eh?"

"Sure. Like bughouse." Presto nodded.

"Who would it be?"

Presto pointed at the town. "Eef that ees Mexico City," he said, "she ees us that ees crazy."

Rush opened his mouth, then suddenly looked like a man who had tasted a lemon.

"That," he said queerly, "isn't Mexico City?"

"She ees ain't."

Rush swallowed, ran a finger inside his collar; then he took out a brown handkerchief and blotted himself. "What," he asked, "is it?"

"Shee's El Paso, *señor.*"

"El Paso, Texas? Texas!"

"Ees best damn town in Texas," Presto said proudly.

"*Oof!*" Rush said.

The short man peered at him. "What?"

"Just—*oof!*" Rush said.

THE TAXICAB was a flivver considered a swanky job when it was turned out fifteen years ago complete with self-starter and one-man top. The road was rough, and Presto drove fast; and Rush was kept busy shoving equipment cases off his lap. Kids, goats and people all got out of their way, and dogs apparently came from blocks around to chase the old hack and bark.

Rush rode the bucking seat, juggled cases and looked at the houses in an exasperated way. This was the Mexican quarter, of course. He began to notice something unusual.

Fully half the houses seemed to have black crape fastened to doorknobs or tied to window bars.

Rush pointed at the crape. "Epidemic in town, or something?"

"*Señor* Juan Madarro ees dead," Presto explained.

Rush settled back and thought about his own troubles. Taking the plane from Miami to Mexico City had seemed a clever move. He'd worn a disguise, departed his Miami hotel by the back door, even booked passage as "Mr. Dunn." He was Mr. Dunn, who was *done.* The pun had seemed appropriate. But apparently he was not as done as he had figured. He began to have a black suspicion that he had not been fast enough on his feet.

His neck should be red. El Paso, Texas, and he had thought it was Mexico City! The pilot of that plane had done a smooth job. The ship had crossed what Rush had thought about the right amount of Gulf of Mexico, and traversed what he took to be the correct amount of land. It was the mountains. The mountains had fooled him. He had heard there were mountains around Mexico City, and there happened to be some sizable hills around El Paso. Rush scowled at the big, dark hills.

The town got better, the streets cleaner, the buildings larger; but it was still the Mexican district when the cab stopped in front of a white structure with iron-railed balconies, bright awnings and a brilliant, green tile roof. The sign said:

AMERICAN HOTEL.

Two large bows of black crape on either side of the door made a strange contrast.

Rush asked, "This a good hotel?"

The driver said, "Sure. Hees best damn hotel in town."

Rush pointed at the black crape. "For *Señor* Juan Madarro?"

"Sure."

"What did this *Señor* Madarro die of?"

"A bullet, *señor*."

"He got shot?"

"Sure."

"What for?"

Presto got out of the car. "Thees best damn hotel in town," he said.

The hotel proprietor was a tall brown man with small bags under each eye and a larger bag for a stomach. After he peered at Rush, he grinned with large white teeth. "Ah, the *Señor* Clickell Rush." He sounded happy. "We have reserve best room in place for you."

"Reserved?"

"Yes."

Rush yelled, *"Who reserved it?"*

The hotel proprietor shrugged. *"Quien sabe?* There is telephone call. Somebody say reserve best room for *Señor* Clickell Rush. He describe you."

"What," Rush asked, "did this telephone voice sound like?"

"She's a little hard to understand, *señor*."

"You've got something there."

"Eh?"

"Hard to understand—you said it!" Rush made fists of his hands and put the fists in his pockets. "Where's this room?"

The room was large, clean and full of coolness. The taxi driver, Presto, helped carry the gadget cases up; then he stood around looking concerned about Rush.

"You ees feel well, *señor?*"

Rush said, "I don't feel as clever as I did."

"Maybe you ees need doctor, no?"

"What I need," Rush said, "is a magician."

"Magician?"

"Somebody to give lessons on disappearing."

Presto left, looking resigned to being puzzled, and Rush sank in a chair and looked angry.

The "Gadget Man" wore a brown linen suit, brown tie, brown handkerchief in his upper coat pocket; his shoes were brown, so was his wrist-watch band. He liked browns.

His height was average, but he did not give the effect of being average, being over-sinewed, his muscles too developed, too trained; so that he looked like a man who might start doing acrobatic stunts at any moment. It usually made lazy people nervous to be around him.

He shut the door, locked it, got his hat off the bed and hung it over the knob to cover the keyhole; then he closed the Venetian blinds on the window. After which, he went around the room looking in things and under things.

The piece of paper was under the base of the table lamp when he lifted it. On it two words were typewritten. They read:

LET'S TALK.

Rush walked twice around the room shaking both fists. He kicked the bed. He kicked a chair. Then he sat down in another chair and said things until he felt better.

Bufa, the toad, was in one of his equipment cases.

The toad had a gaping red mouth of about a size to take a man's fist. The whole toad would fit into a suitcase of good size, with enough room left over for cotton padding. It had warts, the eyes of a tomcat, and a moss-colored back.

It took some maneuvering to get the lighted bulb of the floor lamp into the toad's mouth. When the toad made a humming sound, Rush knew heat from the lighted bulb had caused the thermostat in the toad's mouth to close and turn on the wired-radio "transceiver" inside the toad. He had dissected Bufa often enough to know all about its internal functions.

AT ONE time he had hoped, by tracing parts of the apparatus to the manufacturer, to learn who had constructed the toad. Considering that he had devoted several months of more or less sporadic effort to finding who had made the toad, and who talked through it, he was not proud of results—results being exactly nothing.

He'd merely succeeded in convincing himself that, whoever the voice of the toad was, he or she was clever. He wasn't even sure whether it was man or woman, the voice being disguised always.

He had also convinced himself that the unknown had more money than sense. Undeniably, the unknown was eccentric. Take, for instance, the time six months ago when Rush had turned up in New York City and tried to sell the police department a litter of scientific gadgets which he had invented to catch crooks. Rush had over a thousand gadgets for sale at the time, but the police didn't consider them very practical. Maybe they weren't, generally speaking. It was a matter of opinion.

First Rush heard of the voice of Bufa, he found the toad in his room, sitting on one half of a ten-thousand-dollar bill. From another "transceiver" somewhere in the city, the voice of the toad suggested that Rush solve a particular crime, after which he'd receive the other half of the bill. He'd done so, and got paid. The same thing had happened again. It kept happening. Rush got tired. He'd been trying to quit.

The whole thing was crazy.

But there was no half of a ten-thousand-dollar bill with the note this time. That did not surprise him. In Miami, he'd saved a fortune in cash being smuggled out of Europe, and the owner of the money had presented twenty-five thousand dollars in reward; after which, to Rush's astonishment, the voice of the toad had demanded the reward. Rush, it seemed, was to get ten thousand dollars per case and no more.

Rush refused, and left for Mexico City by plane, taking the toad, inside which the twenty-five thousand dollars, in large bills, was concealed.

He had expected to disappear and enjoy luxury.

But he was in El Paso.

Bufa, the toad, said, *"Rather nice trip, wasn't it? Little surprise at the end, and everything."*

This time, the voice sounded as if it was being disguised by talking through a comb with tissue paper over it.

CHAPTER 11
FLOWERS FOR A SEÑOR

RUSH RESISTED AN impulse to pick up a chair and see what it would do to the toad. The thing always affected him that way.

He said, "You bought 'em off, eh?"

"Bought who?"

"Pilot of that plane!"

The toad said, *"Just between us two, it was rather expensive."*

"So you *did* buy them off!" Rush bent close to the toad to yell, "What's this crazy business all about?"

The toad said, *"Flowers."*

"What flowers?"

"Flowers you will buy at El Flora *flower shop and put in the casket of Señor Juan Madarro."*

Rush said, astonished, "I'm to put some flowers on the grave of this Madarro."

"Not on his grave, exactly. In his casket."

"In it?"

"Inside the casket, yes."

For his next two efforts to speak, Rush only got noises. But finally: "You mean you bribed the plane to drop me here just to put flowers in the casket of somebody I don't even know?"

The toad said, *"Yes."*

Rush said, "It sure makes sense!" through his teeth.

"Of course," the toad added, *"you really trade your flowers for some you will find in the casket."*

"Trade flowers?"

"And in case there is more than one bouquet in the casket, you can feel of them all to see which one you want."

"Feel?"

"Feel for the little mud man."

"Look!" Rush said. "Wait a minute!"

He went into the bathroom and got a drink of water; then took a chair, placed it beside the table on which the toad stood, sat down in the chair and held his head.

He said, "I knew it would be crazy. It always is. So I could stomach the airplane business. I could understand that. You're crazy as a loon. So I understood that. And the flowers, I could stand. It's the thing to put flowers on a man's grave. It's only crazy to put flowers on the grave of somebody you never heard of until to-day. But I could still stand that." He crashed a fist on the table. "But the little mud man is too much!" he yelled.

THE TOAD seemed unperturbed. *"You will buy a little mud man and put him in the flowers which you take to the grave of Madarro."*

Rush asked, "How many little mud men are there?"

"Two. One you buy. The other will be in the flowers already in Madarro's casket."

"I buy this little mud man, eh?"

"Correct."

"What do I ask for?"

"Merely ask for a little mud man."

"Ask where?"

"El Flora *flower shop will do."*

"And after I trade my flowers and little mud man for the flowers and little mud man in Juan Madarro's casket, what happens?"

The toad said, *"You use your own judgment."*

"You mean I'll get in a lot of trouble, don't you?"

"If you do, you'll get paid ten thousand dollars."

Rush said, "I've got ten thousand dollars. I've got two and a half times ten thousand dollars."

"But—"

"That's a lot of money!" Rush interrupted. "It's all the money I need. So you know where you can go jump."

"You refuse this time?"

"With vim and vigor, I refuse."

"Because you've got twenty-five thousand dollars?"

"You bet."

The toad laughed heartily.

"That's what you think. Or didn't you read all my note?"

Like a number of the great shocks of history, that one took a moment to sink in. Rush sat for all of twenty seconds wondering what the crack meant. When it hit him, he lifted out of his chair as if on strings. He stumbled to the note, turned it over, and he read what was on the other side:

RECEIVED PAYMENT, $25,000.00
(SIGNED) BUFA.

Rush got back to the toad with one wild jump. It was not hard to open the toad base in a hurry, and he did that.

The twenty-five thousand dollars which he had hidden there in Miami was gone.

He snarled a string of "Hellos!" to the toad.

There was no answer to any of them. The other "transceiver" had been switched off.

THE *EL FLORA* flower shop had a neon sign, a palm tree on each side of the door, and nice smells came out of the place.

Rush looked around the shop, then said, "I want one little mud man."

The proprietor wore his red hair very slick and spoke slangy English.

He said, "Sure, pal. One little mud guy."

The mud man was of baked clay, the size of a big fist, and had a human shape after a vague fashion. It was not like a Buddha statue, for Buddhas sit with legs crossed—whereas this one just sat.

"Four bits," the flower shop man said. "And it's a bargain at the price."

Rush turned the little mud man various ways in his hands. "What's this piece of brick supposed to be?"

"Some idol or something or other. I think it's Kukul-can—you know, the old-time feathered serpent idol. The Indians and Mexicans buy them, mostly."

"I wonder what for?"

"Well—eh—for the same reason you and me buy a valentine, I guess!"

Rush turned the little mud man over and over, and tried to scratch its fat stomach with a finger nail. The finger nail bent. "Got a hammer?" he queried.

The flower man got a hammer, and Rush put the little mud man on the floor, hit with the hammer and pieces flew all directions. Rush inspected the pieces until he was sure there had been nothing inside the little mud man but baked clay.

"That'll cost you," the flower man said.

"Sure. I'm just suspicious, I reckon. I'll have to have another one. And I want some flowers suitable for *Señor* Juan Madarro's grave. What would you suggest?"

The flower man looked strange. "For who?"

"Madarro?"

"Oh." The other looked even queerer.

"What *was* this Juan Madarro, anyway?" Rush asked.

The flower man began gathering flowers and chopping the stems with the big knife; but after a moment, he put down what flowers he held and got out a cigarette and lighted it, taking plenty of time.

"Madarro," he said finally. "Why—he was a Mexican who died, didn't you say?"

Rush said, "I see. Or do I?"

The flower man swallowed, then picked up his flowers as if in a hurry to be doing something else. He chopped stems, arranged the flowers, tied them with funereal colors, and put them in a box.

He said, "Four dollars and a quarter."

"How about talking some more about Madarro?"

The man licked his lips. "You've got me wrong. I never heard of the man before."

"But—"

The flower man said, "Get out of here!"

"But look—"

The man went over and got the knife he had used on the flower stems, held the blade ready to chop, and came toward Rush. The knife blade was as long as the man's arm from knuckles to elbow, and edged like a razor.

He gritted, "Get out!"

"Oh, my stars!" Rush said.

He got out with his flowers and his little mud man.

ENTERING A taxicab in front of *El Flora* flower shop, Rush said, "The Mexican Cemetery," and the taxi began to move.

Rush opened the flower box, unbound the flowers and retied them so that they surrounded and hid the small semi-manlike statue which looked if it were composed of a poor quality of red brick.

"Damn fool business!" he complained.

Streets got narrower, holes got deeper and the taxi ran faster and faster. The driver put one hand on the horn, kept it there, and kids and pedestrians fled for their lives. The taxi was pursued by a swirl of dust and dogs.

Rush grasped the back of the front seat with both hands and raised up to take a long look at the face of the driver.

He said, "Lo and behold!"

It was Presto. He looked back and grinned.

"Hello!" he yelled.

"Don't you know," Rush shouted, "that it's bad manners to follow people around?"

Presto yanked the steering wheel, stamped at his brakes, and the old car went up on two wheels while the tires made the noises of several pigs. Having rounded the corner, the machine settled back on four wheels.

Presto yelled, "I teenk maybe you ees want to go to Mexico City in toxi-scrab."

"I can see," Rush said, "why they call you 'That Damn Presto.'"

CHAPTER III

THE MUD MEN

THE CEMETERY WALL was like a bolt of second-hand canvas unrolled and stood on edge, and it was unbroken except for the gatehouse, which was massive and arched to form a belfry in which two corroded iron bells hung from wooden cradles that probably could be rocked by a fuzzy rope. The rope ran down and fastened to a peg inside the two iron gates.

"I charge two dollars," Presto explained. "She ees worth five."

"She ees worth about thirty cents," Rush said sourly. "You, the car, and the ride."

"Huh?"

"Look, Presto: I'm usually ashamed to tell people this, but I've got to tell it to you for your own protection. You see, you have such nice white teeth."

"Teeth?"

"Such very nice teeth. Any elephant would be proud of them."

"You ees tenk so?"

"It's too bad, too," Rush said. "Because, when I meet a person the third time the same day, I have to pull out his teeth. I can't help it. It's one of those things. I use pliers."

Presto swallowed. "You know what I teenk? I teenk you ees crazy."

Rush parted with two dollars. "Remember the teeth."

After Presto drove off looking tooth-conscious, Rush carried the box of flowers to the cemetery gate and called, "Hey!" without getting an answer. After he had called, "Hey!" three or four times, he grasped the massive gate to give it a shaking. But the gate was too heavy for him to have much success, so he maneuvered until he could get his hand through the bars and clutch and yank the bell rope. This caused an astonishing racket.

A long-looking man came and looked through the gate.

"*Que quiere?*" he muttered.

Rush said, "Know English?"

"What do you want?" the man asked in good-enough English.

Rush explained that he had flowers for the casket of Madarro.

The long man said, "I'll take them. I am the caretaker here."

"I'll place them myself."

The long man frowned. "Impossible."

Rush wondered how much the long man would miss being twice as tall as himself, or if that was partly the effect of the gate steelwork. The fellow was tall enough to look almost comical.

Rush said, "Impossible, eh?"

"*Sí.*"

"That's too bad. Ah—could you point out Juan Madarro's grave from here?"

The long man hesitated. "The black one yonder," he said finally, and slanted an arm at a tomb that was a plain cube, nearly a score of feet square, made of jet-black stone that had been polished until it was like an ebony mirror.

"Thanks," Rush said. "And you won't let me in?"

"No."

Rush fished in pockets as though in search of bribe money. When he had fished for some moments, he dropped the box of flowers, apparently by accident. Doubling over for them, he placed under his right shoe the small glass bottle which he had taken from a pocket.

"Sort of clumsy, eh?" He looked embarrassed. "Well, thanks. I guess we'll let the whole thing drop."

He ground his right foot down on the bottle in turning, coughed to hide noise of the glass being crushed. Then he walked away for fifty yards or so, waited two or three minutes for the breeze to take away the gas he had liberated.

He went back. The gas from the bottle had made the long man unconscious by then.

RUSH REACHED through the gate for the long man's trouser leg, and after three failures, pulled the fellow close enough to go through his pockets. He unearthed a key which looked massive enough to belong to the gate lock, used the key; it took hard pushing to get the gate open. He examined the long man, because any gas capable of producing unconsciousness so abruptly was a shock to the human system, and there was always a possibility that a victim might need a stimulant.

The long man had long ears, and black hair grew down on his forehead in a wedge; the general effect was devilish. His eyebrow hairs were extraordinarily long.

Satisfied the man was unharmed, Rush went on toward the tomb, carrying his box of flowers.

The tomb looked as square as anything could be made, with no seam or joint visible anywhere, nor any ornamentation of any kind except a name cut into the black smoothness over the door. It said:

MADARRO

Rush went close to the shiny blackness and looked vainly for seams. He made fingerprints on the cool stone, and they faded as fingerprints left on a mirror by a warm hand will fade. The stone must have come from abroad, and the workmanship was fantastic. Rush said, "Half a million dollars, anyhow," and thereafter had respect for the financial standing of the Madarros.

He walked through the tomb door into utter stillness and the smell of flowers. The patch of white light from his flashlight wandered like a ghost over caskets in wall receivers. It was a family tomb. Juan Madarro's casket stood in a lake of flowers in the center of the tomb.

Before he opened the casket, Rush breathed in and out deeply three or four times, began perspiring, and took a tight hold on his lower lip with his teeth. He did not like this. After he got the lid up, the fact that Juan Madarro was a natural-looking corpse did not help any, either.

There was one bunch of flowers inside the casket.

Rush took them and substituted his own; then he backed out into the sunlight and looked at the backs of his hands. They were damp. His brown shirt on either side of his necktie was wet with perspiration, and he felt as if sweat had puddled in his armpits.

He said, "The life of a grave-robber!" wryly.

Then he blotted accessible parts of his anatomy with a handkerchief, flopped his coat open and shut to get cool air inside, and fanned with his hat. Having gotten back something like normal feeling, he felt around in the flowers distastefully until he found a little mud man. The mud man was not exactly like the one he had bought—this one was somewhat better made.

He turned the mud man, examined it, and was deciding there seemed to be nothing peculiar about it, when the girl shot him.

ALWAYS THEREAFTER, he knew there was no surprise quite equal to being unexpectedly shot.

Impact of the bullet against his ribs, and powder noise from the gun were about simultaneous. The gun roar scared up birds all over the cemetery; the bullet pushed him off balance. Because he tried to use his hands to hold the little mud man instead of to break his fall, he rooted the ground with his face. The mud man rolled off somewhere.

He thought of several things in practically no time at all. First, it was fortunate the girl had kept her head and shot at the bigger target of his body, instead of his head, for there was an alloy mesh armor protecting his body, and nothing at all to protect his head.

The armor was one of his gadgets, and he always used it when there was possibility of trouble. Thinking did not interfere with his rolling; but to the solid black corner of the tomb seemed a mile before he made it.

He was glad the Mexicans planted plenty of shrubbery in their cemeteries. Having hurdled the first clump, he got down on all fours and scrambled, changing directions. A bullet went through the brush, made chopping noises, hit a tombstone and climbed, sounding as if someone had given a flute a hard puff.

Rush took from his clothing a mirror similar to those which dentists use to look at teeth, but with a telescoping handle that would run out as long as his arm. He stretched the handle, lay on his back and used the mirror as a periscope.

The girl wore black and white. Her frock was black, with white at belt and collar. She was small, dark, with a startlingly white face and black, shiny hair pulled back in a tight, unbecoming way. The only color other than black and white about her, was her lips. In spite of that, she was pretty; particularly, there was something about her mouth. She looked tiny and pale and like a nun, all but her mouth.

She kept jumping up with her gun ready, looking for something to shoot at. The gun was an automatic, black with gold inlay.

Rush got out another vial of his anaesthetic gas, and threw it. The girl saw it arching toward her, and shot at the spot from which she imagined it had come. Her guess was wrong by not more than six feet. The gas fell short. The girl began shooting at the mirror. Rush changed position.

When he put the mirror up again, the small dark girl was seizing the little mud man. She straightened and ran toward the cemetery gate, mud man in one hand, gun in the other hand.

Rush threw two more bottles of his anaesthetic gas, and both fell short. He made a mental note after this to carry one or two weighted bottles, for throwing.

He tried yelling, "Stop!" But that was much too success-ful—the girl promptly halted, turned, and shot at him.

After she ran through the cemetery gate, she veered right, in a way that showed she knew where she was going. Rush used caution following her, and reached the gate in time to see a small black coupé leave in haste, with the pugilistic girl at the wheel.

RUSH MADE disgusted noises. Black coupés of that descrip-tion were as common as blue serge suits. And the license plates had been smeared with mud.

He went back to the long man who lay inside the gate. The fellow was beginning to stir a little, making low noises. Rush closed the gate, locked himself out of the cemetery; then, he reached through the bars, replaced the keys in the long man's pocket. At that point, the man opened his eyes. As an excuse for having his hands on the fellow, Rush began to shake the man as if trying to arouse him.

"Hey!" Rush said. "Wake up!"

The man coughed and made snuffling sounds, then felt of his head with both hands. He tried to sit up, kicking about with both legs, and failed to make it. He rolled over, got on all fours. He said, "Wh—wh—" several times.

Rush said, "It's not your heart, is it?"

"Huh?" The man looked at him. "Heart?"

"Well, from the way you fell over, I didn't know."

The man shut his eyes, kept them shut for several moments; then opened them and without looking directly at Rush, mumbled, "Help me get up, will you?"

"Sure." Rush reached through the gate bars, got both hands under the long man's armpits, and lifted. The man came up slowly, as loose as rope. He made faces. His arms milled around, apparently with no object, until his hands got through the bars, one on either side of Rush's head.

He took hold of Rush's head, jerked it against the bars. Rush saw pain-colored haze.

The man snarled, "Play me for a sap, will you?"

He grabbed Rush's hair with his left hand, set himself. With his right hand, he uppercut Rush's jaw as hard as he could.

Rush fell down where it was remarkably black.

CHAPTER IV

SMOKE

THE VOICES CAME into existence as though a radio was being turned on slowly. At first, they were unnatural, with a background of ringing sound; but, a bit at a time, they became more real.

Rush listened to the voices with immense concentration, and at last he came to the conclusion that they were real voices, and not something his imagination was making. By then, his mind had straightened out the fact that he had been slugged. He started wondering what he was holding with his right hand.

One of the voices complained, "This is damned foolishness!"

Another voice said, "He'll be out of it in a minute, and his reactions will be confused. He'll be dazed. What he says may be of some value."

"I'll bet his face'll be red," surmised a third voice.

Silence followed, and Rush got to wondering again what his right hand was holding. He moved his fingers, feeling. It was round, long, hard. Below it was cloth; under the cloth something that was not hard, nor soft either. Rush got his eyes open and made them focus on the hand.

When he saw he had been holding a knife handle, and that the knife blade was sticking in a man, he made an animal noise, let go the knife, rolled wildly, and tried to come up on his feet.

He did not make it, because the three men who had been talking mashed him out on the ground again.

The three men wore police uniforms. They wrestled with Rush's arms until they got them together and fastened at the wrists with handcuffs. One of the cops slapped Rush twice.

Another cop said, "He don't need that, Earl."

"It'll clear his head," Earl said.

Rush struggled, throwing his weight against the officers, until they let him get up.

The dead man had white hair, wrinkles, and a week's growth of white beard. His age was at least sixty. His overalls and blue shirt had needed washing even before the blood got on them.

Rush said, "Who—uh—who—" and could not make his tongue handle the rest of the question.

"He's the caretaker." Earl, who had slapped Rush, reached out and slapped him again. "An old man twice your age!"

RUSH MUMBLED, "The—caretaker?" and peered at the dead man. It was not the long man who had said he was the caretaker.

One of the policemen clutched a handful of Rush's hair, held his head while he felt of the bruises made when the long man yanked Rush's head against the gate bars.

"The old duffer must've put up a fight at that," the cop said. "But what gets me is the motive."

The cop called Earl snorted. "That's an easy one."

"How do you mean, Earl?"

"Why, this red-hot"—Earl slapped Rush again—"shot Madarro. He figured his bullet was still in Madarro's body, and he wanted it. So he came to get it. The caretaker put up an argument, and there you are."

"Hell, Earl, he'd know they got the bullet at the autopsy."

"How do you know he's got that much brains?" Earl asked. "I've got it figured right. The caretaker gave him a clubbing, and this bird used the knife, then passed out from the clubbing. Somebody saw it and telephoned us."

Rush looked interested and said, "Telephoned you? Someone telephoned you?"

"Sure."

"Who?"

"Wouldn't say. But we traced the call here to the cemetery gatehouse phone."

"Don't you think that's queer?"

"What's queer about it? Lots of people don't like to testify in court."

Rush pinched his eyes together, trying to concentrate. "What gave you the idea I killed Madarro?"

The policeman named Earl laughed and drew a gun from his pocket, an English Webley automatic revolver, an unusual make. "There's not many of these around. And our ballistics department decided that Madarro was shot with one of them."

Rush growled, "What does that prove?"

"You guess."

"Eh?"

"We found it in your pocket," the policeman said.

THE POLICEMAN went around behind and took hold of Rush's coat collar. He said, "We'd better go over him again. I don't think we got all the stuff out of his clothes the first time."

They began searching.

Rush asked, "Who was this *Señor* Juan Madarro, anyway?"

"That," Earl said, "is something else that's got us puzzled. We can't get anything out of the Mexicans. But half the

Mexican houses in town hung out crape after he died."

"Then he was somebody important," Rush decided.

"That's what we're thinking."

Rush frowned. "What about his family? Anything there?"

"Yes and no."

"What do you mean?"

"His sister is something, if you put it one way." Earl grinned a little. "Something I wouldn't mind finding in my sock Christmas morning, I mean."

Rush took in a deep breath, thought about the girl who had taken the little mud man from him and shot at him.

He said, "Her mouth is what you remember about her, isn't it?"

Earl said, "So you know her?"

"Up to now," Rush said sourly, "you can put me down as not knowing anything."

One of the policeman said. "This bulletproof vest he's got on is the damnedest thing. I wonder how you get it off?"

"There's a zipper on the left side," Rush offered.

The policeman found the zipper and stripped it upward roughly. A flat case, which had been under the vest, fell out, its two halves opening like a clam shell. It hit the ground. By the time it had bounced, it was surrounded by a wad of black smoke already the size of a football, and growing.

"Hey!" Earl yelled. "What—"

There was loud hissing as the sepia smoke squirted around and upward for yards. Rush jumped backward against Earl, who held his collar, and he and Earl fell down. On his second twisting effort, Rush got loose. By that time, the smoke had become a pall in which nothing could be seen. Rush got up and ran for the cemetery gate.

With one hand, he worked at the zipper of the bulletproof mesh vest until he got it shut. Under the vest had always been a good place to carry the smoke bomb, which was of necessity as large as a cigarette case. Carrying it so the detonator would trip if anyone but himself took it out, was an incidental idea.

He angled through the gate, took the center of the street, and tried to make his legs get longer. In the cemetery, the cop named Earl began yelling. Mostly he howled that Rush had probably gone through the gate. Rush headed for the nearest street corner, and was going around it when bullets began to go past making noises he would never forget.

There was a taxicab in the side street, rolling slowly enough to let Rush overtake it. When he saw it was empty except for the driver, he landed on the running board, got the door open and swung inside.

"Get going!" he said.

The cab surprised him and got going.

"THE AMERICAN HOTEL," Rush said.

The cab went fast, took side streets, made enough turns to lose any pursuit, and eventually approached the American Hotel.

"There may be an alley you can wait in," Rush said.

There was an alley. The cab went into it and stopped. Rush got out and opened the front door of the machine. He addressed the driver.

"I don't figure you out," he said. "But I think you're worth figuring."

Presto, who was driving the cab, looked innocent. "Believe heem or not," he said, "we have flat tire and stop to feex heem."

Rush said sourly, "Believe heem or not, this won't hurt you—permanently."

Presto was slow dodging, and Rush took him by the neck. They became a knot on the floor of the cab and skinned themselves on the clutch and brake pedals and the gear-shift lever; then they flopped out on the alley pavement and bounced around, finally ending up under the car, where Rush managed to bang Presto's head on the hard drive shaft until the fellow got limp.

Rush threw Presto in the car, puffing, "You've been too Johnny-on-the-spot all along."

He went into the hotel by the back door and saw no one on the way to his room. Carrying two equipment cases, he went back to the car. He placed the cases in the back of the cab. Presto had not moved.

Rush went to his room again and on this second trip, took his time getting stuff together in order to move. After he had idled and listened for about ten minutes, he heard a car go away from the back of the hotel.

Rush went down to the alley.

Presto and the cab were gone.

Rush wore a thin, pleased grin as he went up to the room and distributed in his pockets and clothing such gadgets as he might need, or could carry readily. He had almost finished that job when he discovered something. Something astounding. He stared at his hands.

"Damn!" he said, and realized he must be more excited than he had thought, or he would have noticed it earlier.

There was brown make-up grease paint on his fingers where he had held Presto's neck.

CHAPTER V
RADIO TRAIL

RUSH LEFT THE American Hotel, carrying only one piece of baggage, a suitcase. He had put on wrinkled white linens, black shoes and a soft, white felt hat; the salesman had said the hat could be folded and packed without harming its shape, but that was a piece of misinformation. The hat was awful. Rush carried a cane, and when he got out on the sidewalk, he faked a limp and used the cane.

He walked far enough to get very tired of the fake limp, before he found a rent-a-car place which was a branch of a nation-wide agency. He carried a card from the agency that entitled him to rent a car without the usual preliminaries. He selected a blue coach.

Driving half a dozen blocks, he parked, opened the bag he had brought along, and put on the earphones connected to the directional radio receiver which it contained. There was a folding loop aerial which plugged in the top of the device. He put that in place, and switched the set on. Shortly, he was hearing a short buzzing note which came with clockwork ten-second regularity.

Buzzing was loudest when he set the loop northeast by southwest. He drove southwest for about twenty blocks, then decided the buzzing was getting weaker, meaning he was going the wrong direction. He turned around and drove northeast.

It was a warm afternoon. Hot-tamale men had shoved carts into the shade and were resting on their little stools. There were no kids or dogs in the street. Women carried fans. The buzzing in the radio direction-finder slowly got louder.

He passed the park in the center of El Paso, with its benches and pleasant trees, dividing his attention between watching traffic and listening to the radio. After a while, the traffic thinned, and he drove on a wide boulevard where the houses became pretentious.

Presto's old taxicab stood beside a high, snow-white wall. Fresh-looking green shrubbery stood beyond the wall, and in the shrubbery was an expanse of bright, tile roof. There had not been a more impressive house on the street. An unusually tall flagpole stood on the house.

Presto was not in the cab. The cases Rush had put in the back were still there. One contained the radio transmitter that had been sending out the signal which the direction-finder had located. The lid of that one stood open.

The note lying on the transmitter said:

YOU WOULD HAVE DECIDED THIS WAS
THE PLACE, ANYWAY.

Rush said, "I would, eh? *Hm-m-m.*"

He stood there and changed from one foot to the other, as if the ground did not feel very solid. To begin with, he had been mystified when the plane put him off in El Paso instead of Mexico City. He had seen no sense to that. Then he had seen no sense in practically anything that had happened afterward.

In a general way, it might be logical. A man of mystery named Madarro had been murdered, and there was something important in his casket. A mud man. What made a mud man important remained to be seen. But it must be important. The long man had been at the cemetery to get it, probably, and he had murdered the caretaker and hidden the body. Then Rush had come along and got the little mud man, and Madarro's sister had taken it from him. Then the long man had tried to get rid of Rush, by framing him for the caretaker's murder.

Rush took a deep breath. When you looked at it that way, it did make some sense.

All but Presto. He didn't make any sense at all. Presto wasn't any Mexican.

THE WHITE wall was high enough that Rush had to leap four times, and scrape hide off his right wrist, before he got an arm hooked over the top. After that, it was easy to get over to the other side. He stood in flowers up to his neck, listening and hearing nothing, then went toward the house.

The flagpole was even taller than it had seemed. It was a very fat flagpole. Almost too much flagpole.

All lower windows of the house were barred, after the Spanish way, with bars that were effective as well as ornamental. Bright awnings were held out from the windows by iron spears. There was a patio in the center, and an automobile drive passed into this patio through high metal gates which had a lock too complicated to take time to pick. All doors seemed to be locked.

Rush looked into a window, and made sure the room inside was empty. He faced away from the house, reached up and grasped the lower edge of an awning. Slowly, like an acrobat "skinning the cat," he brought his legs up, then his body, until he lay on the awning. He squirmed until he made the awning pocket enough to hold him. From there, he could reach a second-floor window which was not barred.

That room was empty. He went through other rooms

that were empty except for rich furniture, until he found the room under the flagpole. He was interested in that flagpole.

The flagpole came down through the upstairs room disguised as an ornamental column.

In the ground floor room, it was also disguised as a column.

Rush went into the basement, still tracing the flagpole. He was as quiet as he could be about it. He found game rooms and a laundry full of stuff that is in laundries, and a room where there was an air-conditioning unit. Then a storeroom walled completely with plank shelves, and cold with refrigerated air.

From the ceiling hung game, mostly birds, two lambs and a quartered beef. The food on the shelves was mostly the hot stuff Mexicans like in their food, and bottled wines.

Rush was absently reading wine labels, when there was a scraping noise—and a section of the wall and shelves started swinging out.

He got out of the room with haste and hid behind the air-conditioning unit.

The long man of the cemetery came out of the storeroom. He did not look right or left, but went upstairs.

RUSH WENT into the storeroom and through the open, hidden door with a tear-gas bomb in each hand. He was then in a place of pale light and much electrical machinery. He saw identical sets of motor-dynamos, two high-powered radio panels which were twins with meters and dials and knobs, and a table on which stood a loud-speaker and a canlike condenser microphone on a desk stand.

To the left was a workbench, on which stood an electric drill, four little mud men with holes half an inch in diameter drilled in them, and a glass jar obviously containing a compound, looking exactly like the bricklike baked clay of the mud men, for sealing the holes so as not to be notice-able. There were a hundred or so little mud men on a shelf over the bench, and under the bench a box containing the parts of little mud men which had been broken.

In another corner stood empty boxes, in some of which paper was stuffed.

Rush went to that corner when the long man came back. He got down behind the boxes.

The long man was still in a great hurry. He carried a pair of pliers and a skillet. He put pliers and skillet on the bench, took a fistful of pistol cartridges from his coat pocket and put those on the bench.

He began pulling the bullets out of the brass cartridge cases with the pliers. He poured the powder into the skillet. When he had emptied all the cartridges, he picked up the skillet containing the powder and walked around to the side of the radio outfit.

He was out of sight behind the equipment a moment; then appeared again. He was examining the radio in a way that showed he knew something about such things. He peered at the transmitter bulbs.

"Five hundred watts," he said.

He scowled at someone on the other side of the radio panels, someone Rush had not noticed.

The man said, "No wonder Madarro was always up on what was going on in Mexico City." He touched the radio. "The aerial inside that flagpole. That's nice, too. Is the outfit in Mexico City as good as this one?"

Whomever he spoke to gave no answer.

"Is it?" he snapped.

No answer.

The long man showed his teeth in an unpleasant way.

"You're not doing yourself any good, acting like this," he said. "We were as much a part of the organization as

Madarro was. He was the leader. We followed. That was the only difference."

The man made an angry sound. "Hell, that wasn't the only difference. Madarro wanted to get results with politics. He kept insisting on no assassinations. No shootings. No bloodshed. Damn, we got tired of that!" He made his angry sound again. "The only way to get that government in Mexico City out of power is with guns!"

Rush saw now that the fellow was a fanatic. The man's long arms went up with the drama of a radical on a soap box.

"Guns!" he shouted. "Assassinate the leaders! Bomb their homes! Bomb their supporters! That's the way!"

His fire subsided.

"That's the way it's going to be done, too," he said grimly, "now that we have the milksop, Madarro, out of the way."

He got hold of the figure behind the radio equipment and dragged it out where there was more light, and where Rush could see. It was the girl with the mouth, the Madarro girl.

Rush got a small green-paper-wrapped package out of his clothing.

THE LONG man stripped down the stocking on the girl's right leg, holding the leg by pressing a knee on it. The girl was bound. The man put a little pile of the gunpowder from the cartridge on her leg, and got matches out of his pockets.

"Now," he said, "there's one thing we've got to have. That's the roll."

The girl glared at him, and jerked around, and shook the gunpowder off her leg.

"I do not know what you're talking about!"

The man snorted. "Hell you don't! The roll. The list of men in our organization."

"You're crazy!"

"We've got to have it," the long man said doggedly. "It's the finest revolutionary organization anybody ever developed in Mexico. We get the names, and we can carry on with the organization. If we don't get them—"

He made ugly noises, put more powder on the girl's leg and struck a match. He gritted, "Out with it!"

The girl screamed, and did not run out of breath until the match had burned short in the man's hand. He struck another match.

He yelled, "You tried to bury it with him! You wanted to bust up the organization. We figured that out! Now where is it?"

Rush placed his little green package on one of the boxes. Then he charged.

The long man would have put the match to the powder if Rush had not hit him. Rush hit with too much enthusiasm, and like many men who try to do things in too big a way, he fell short. His fist scraped the man's head and merely upset the fellow.

The man was good with his long legs, and instantly upset Rush with them; then the legs got around Rush like pythons. Rush hit the man. The man hit back. He also got a finger in Rush's left eye. Rush took hold of the other's arm, held the arm so the man could not dodge, and landed what he ever afterward believed to be the hardest blow he ever struck in his life.

Rush got up and tried to say, "Wouldn't Joe Louis be a sucker for that one!" but the words, distorted with his hard breathing, were only noise.

The girl said, "Someone is coming!"

It was the flower shop man. He came down the basement steps carrying a large armful of bright flowers, saying, "Here's some flowers somebody ordered, and I hope it was all right to breeze right in here— What the hell!"

He stopped.

Rush said, "I'll take the flowers," and walked forward.

The flower man looked the basement over well enough to be sure there was no one but Rush, the girl and the unconscious long man.

"You won't take anything!" he said harshly.

Rush halted. "Yeah," he said, "flower shops usually deliver in boxes, don't they? Yours aren't in a box. And all the outside doors were locked, anyway."

The flower man shook his flowers away from the gun which he had been carrying in his right hand, concealed in the bouquet. He pointed the gun at Rush.

"That's right," he said.

RUSH PUT his hands up and began talking in a long-winded, soothing way. He said, "You fellows will need some money to go ahead with this revolution you're going to stage in Mexico, and you know as well as I do that the thing is best worked from a headquarters on this side of the border, because the secret police in Mexico are not slouches at ferreting out things of this kind, and a headquarters like this costs money to keep going. We might get together on that, because I'm not an American Federal agent, or a Mexican secret agent, or anything like that, and if you'll give me a chance to explain, I might also do something about the list of names that you're so anxious about. You see, the girl put it in one of the little mud men and put it in her brother's casket; and then—"

What he had been waiting for happened. There was a flash. It was utterly blinding. It came from the box where Rush had put the green package. It was a sustained flash, lasting ten seconds or so. It made such light that looking anywhere in the room was like staring at a welding-torch flame. It was entirely blinding.

Rush hit the flower man about the time the flash was

dying out. He hit the man just above the belt; hit him with all his might and much pleasure. Air through the flower man's teeth sounded as if someone had tried to blow a bugle. He fell down, and did not need to be hit the second time.

Rush hit him anyway.

THE POLICE were patient enough—they listened, at least. They listened patiently for two hours; after that, getting a little desperate, Rush asked for and received permission to talk to Alondra Madarro—her name was Alondra—alone.

He thought he was rather eloquent with the girl for half an hour. He thought he did rather well.

"No," she said. "I won't give you a date."

Rush went out and said to the policemen, "No gratitude at all."

"You mean she wouldn't talk?" Earl demanded.

"Talk? Who said anything about talk?" Rush sighed. "Oh, she talked a little. It was one of those revolution things. Exiles scheming to overthrow the government that had exiled them. They had quite an organization. Lots of El Paso Mexicans in it. Remember how many doors had crape on them when Madarro died? Let's see what else she said. Oh, yes. The little mud men. They used those to pass written orders around. That *El Flora* flower shop was the clearing house for orders. The proprietor was one of the organization, of course. He helped kill Madarro, too. Madarro was killed because he was too cautious, and was making everybody else be cautious."

The cop named Earl came over and poked Rush in the chest with a finger.

"Got quite a rep in the East, ain't you?" he said.

"Eh?"

"We looked you up. You're called the Gadget Man. Take that gimmick with a timer in it, that you left on the box in the basement, to help out in case you got the little end of your fight. That's an example."

"Want to buy it?" Rush looked interested. "Say, I've got a lot of such things to sell to you cops—"

"Hell with that," Earl said. "What we want to know is how you got mixed in this."

"Oh, that."

"Yes. How'd you come to show up?"

"It was purely involuntary," Rush said. "Purely."

"That don't make sense."

"I'll say it didn't." Rush got his hat. "You through with me?"

"I hope so," Earl said disgustedly.

Rush went back to his hotel.

There was a note lying on top of a pile of clothes on the table. It read:

DON'T YOU THINK I MADE A GOOD MEXI-CAN?

BUFA.

The clothes were the ones Presto, the taxi driver, had worn. Under the clothes was a glass jar containing brown theatrical grease paint, and a bottle containing black hair dye.

Jar and bottle were sitting on a ten-thousand-dollar bill.

Printed in the USA
CPSIA information can be obtained
at www.ICGtesting.com
LVHW050237190923
758386LV00120B/378